A Re

Jenika Snow

A Real Man: Volume One
By Jenika Snow
www.JenikaSnow.com
Jenika_Snow@Yahoo.com
Copyright © September 2016 by Jenika Snow
First E-book Publication: September 2016
Photographer: Wander Aguiar :: Photography
Model: Marshall Perrin
Photo provided by: Wander Book Club

USA Today Bestselling Author

Jenika Snow

Real men always
do it better...

A Real Man

Volume One

A Real Man Series

Book 1: Lumberjack
Book 2: Virgin
Book 3: Baby Fever
Book 4: Experienced (Coming September)

LUMBERJACK

A Real Man, 1

LUMBERJACK (A Real Man, 1)

By Jenika Snow

www.JenikaSnow.com

Jenika_Snow@Yahoo.com

Copyright © June 2016 by Jenika Snow

First E-book Publication: June 2016

She hasn't been with
a real man ... until now.

LUMBERJACK
A Real Man

USA TODAY BESTSELLING AUTHOR
Jenika Snow

He hasn't been with a woman in five years.

She hasn't been with a real man ... until now.

Vivian

I've had enough of the crap that goes along with living in the city. So, I packed for a weeklong vacation in the mountains. Isolation in a cabin for the next seven days sounds like a good way to recoup and get my life back in order. After getting lost while hiking, I stumble upon a cabin that has me questioning whether to ask for help, or if I should brave staying the night in the woods.

Jake

I left everything behind years ago after the woman I was with betrayed me. Now I work as a lumberjack and live my life as a recluse. Being celibate for the last five years says a lot about my self-control, but I'm a man and have needs, and not giving into what I really want is hard as hell. But I can't let myself get close to anyone, not even for a few hours. Getting close is how I got screwed over before.

As soon as I see Vivian, I know I have to have her. It's been forever since I've had a woman. Because of a storm rolling in, she'll have to stay with me overnight. We could do a lot of filthy things in that time. I pride myself on my control, but when it comes to Vivian, I don't know if I can keep my hands to myself.

I know I can't.

I have needs, and it's clear Vivian's in need of a real man to help her unwind. I can certainly help her in that department.

Warning: If you're looking for a sappy, pull-your-heartstring kind of book ... this isn't it. If you want a short and dirty story featuring an all-around alpha hero who hasn't had a woman in years, and a heroine who'll find out what it's like to be with a real man ... this might be for you.

Chapter One

Jake

Sweat beaded on my forehead, but I didn't deviate from my work. My flannel was soaked, as was the white t-shirt underneath it.

I wrapped my arms around the log I'd just chopped down and cut into three separate pieces, hoisted it over my shoulder, and moved toward my chopping block. After dropping the wood on the ground, I pulled my ax from the wooden block, and started going to town on cutting the log into manageable pieces.

I lifted the ax above my head for only a millisecond before bringing it down on the wood in front of me. It splintered in two and fell to the side.

All around me, the sound of men chopping wood and swinging their axes across tree trunks, echoed around the forest. I was focused, because being anything but that during this kind of work was dangerous.

The sound of the lunch horn rang, and I finished chopping the last log. After gathering what I'd cut, I tossed it into the bin and headed over to where the other lumberjacks were.

Men were gathered around with their lunch boxes in their laps, their food already out and being shoveled into their faces. I sat down on a log away from everyone and took out my sandwich. The sound of the machines running in the distance and the logs dropping into the water filled my head. This is what I'd done for the last five years.

Moving out in the middle of nowhere had been the only thing I could think of doing to get away from my toxic life. After I caught my girlfriend fucking my best friend, I'd cleaned out my bank account, packed the shit that meant anything to me, and left.

Truth was I'd been unhappy in my life anyway, and I'd needed a good kick in the ass to get me moving and leaving all that shit behind.

So, I'd done just that. I told my family what I was doing, and where I'd be if they needed me. Then I went off the grid, thinking about me for once, getting my shit in order.

That seemed like a lifetime ago now, but here I was: still loving every fucking minute of it.

"Jake, you coming to town with us tonight?"

I looked over at one of the men I'd worked with for only a year.

"No," was all I said and finished eating.

"After all these years of us asking you to come with us, find some women, and let off steam, why do you always say no?"

I stared at Bruce— I'd worked with him since becoming a lumberjack. Bruce had been with the company for years before I came along, and although he was a hard worker, I'd never seen him as a friend.

Hell, I didn't see anyone a friend, not really.

I kept to myself, did my work, and when my shift was over, I headed home and lived in solitude.

"Because I like my isolation," was all I said.

"Or maybe you like to jerk off?" One of the newer guys, a younger man who was a prick, said.

I didn't bother responding; I'd learned long ago I needed to keep to myself and not let shit get me worked up. The only thing violence ever solved for me was a momentary pleasure, like when I'd knocked my best friend's teeth in after he pulled his dick out of my girlfriend.

I hadn't gotten into a fight since.

After I finished my sandwich and the lunch horn rang again, I got back to work. The sweat had cooled on my body, but I'd work up another one in a few minutes.

And I sure as hell did jerk off. Not being with a woman might be my choice because I didn't want to socialize with anyone, but I wasn't going to get blue balls because I was stubborn.

Fuck that.

I'd worry about myself, force myself not to react to some asshole's jabs, and focus on why I'd come out here in the first place ... to get away from all the bullshit.

Vivian

"This is bullshit, Viv."

I didn't bother looking at Russ as he all but shouted right in my face.

"Back off, Russ." I was annoyed, and I couldn't be held liable for my reaction if he didn't give me the personal space I fucking wanted.

"Viv—"

"Just stop," I said and turned around, facing the man I'd just broken it off with. "We have only been together for three months, and in that time you've fucked your way through the office and managed to bitch about anything and everything. You and I both know whatever we were doing with each other wasn't going to last. It wasn't real." I rubbed my head, feeling so damn tired all of the sudden. "I'm twenty-nine years old. I'm not staying in a relationship—or whatever the hell we've had—when it isn't going anywhere."

Russ cocked his head back like I'd just slapped him.

"Excuse me?" he said with shock and disgust in his voice.

"Yeah, Russ, I know about you sticking your dick in anything that has a hole."

He snapped his mouth shut after I said that. Had he really not wondered why we'd only had sex a handful of time since we'd been dating? Hell, I hadn't even let him touch me after I found out he'd been banging half the office.

He straightened and narrowed his eyes. "We didn't have an exclusive relationship, Vivian."

I snorted at that comment. True, we hadn't actually said those words, but hell, when I slept with a man, and went on dates with him, I thought that meant we wouldn't be going around screwing everyone.

I didn't bother responding; I just exhaled and shook my head.

"Come on, this is crazy," he said and grabbed my arm. I pulled out of his grasp. "Don't fucking touch me, Russ. I asked you to leave, but you're still here. If you say we weren't exclusive, then why in the hell are you still here?" The truth was I hadn't actually seen a future with him anyway. Maybe I'd just stayed with him for this long to entertain the idea of not being a lonely spinster?

He didn't answer right away, but I didn't wait for him to. I walked over to the front door of my apartment, opened it, and glared at him. "It's over. I can't even say it was fun while it lasted, Russ, but it was what it was."

"And it's over, just like that?"

I nodded. "Just like that. Now, please get the hell out of my apartment."

He grumbled something under his breath, but I didn't care if he was cursing me out. I just wanted him gone so I could finish packing.

"Fine." He walked past me, but stopped before he walked out of my place. "And if you weren't such a tight ass, Vivian, maybe things could have worked out."

I just shook my head that he had to get one last dig in.

When he was out of my apartment, I shut and locked the door, and went back over to my suitcase. I needed to get my shit together and hit the road; I planned on disconnecting for the next week. This little trip was definitely a spur of the moment kind of thing, but I knew it would do me good. It had to, because right now I was tired of the world around me.

Taking off work hadn't been difficult since as I was in a top position at the firm where I worked. Although I'd had to rearrange my schedule and place clients on different days, I knew if I didn't do this for myself, I'd go crazy.

I zipped up my bag and sat on the couch. Grabbing my laptop, I looked over reservation I'd made. I was going to spend the next seven days in a cabin three hours from the city. It wasn't a huge leap in the vacation direction, but it sure as hell would be better than what was going on in my life right now. The city noises, sights, lights, and all the bullshit that came with it and my job would fade away as I focused on just me.

Hell, the cabin didn't even have a TV, let alone Wi-Fi, so I would be totally disconnected from everything and everyone, and it's exactly what I needed. Maybe I wouldn't even come back. Maybe I'd find so much peace in the middle of nowhere that I just said fuck everything else.

I wouldn't know until I went, but I was open to just about anything right now.

Chapter Two

Jake

As I headed to my truck after work, I heard the guys talking about going into town and scoring. They were like teenage guys for the way they talked, but I didn't give a fuck. I'd gone the route of treating a woman with respect, and she'd fucked me over royally. Even before her, I had never been one to hit up the bar trying to stick my dick in the easiest female. And I certainly hadn't done that after *her*.

I opened the bed of my truck and grabbed my cloth. After wiping off my ax, I stored it and closed the bed before walking around to the driver's side. I was fucking sweaty and filthy, but I'd worked hard as hell, and being exhausted meant I'd crash for the night instead of lying in bed and thinking about how alone I really was. I might like the peace and quiet, and love the solitude, but the fact remained I also liked women, and not having one in years was pretty fucking hard.

The way they smelled so damn sweet, and the fact they were soft all over, had me harder than steel every damn night. I didn't think about just one female in particular, but just about women in general. I had no hopes of ever finding that perfect woman for me, not where I lived. But I didn't want to open myself up again, not when the last time had ended with me being betrayed by two people I thought had my best interests at heart.

The fact I rarely ventured down the mountain to try and meet a woman certainly didn't help the situation.

No, I might complain about being lonely, but I enjoyed that solitude, too.

I got in my truck and made the forty-five minute drive to my cabin. I was out in the middle of fucking nowhere, having built the cabin two years ago. I'd poured all my savings, and what I'd earned working as a lumberjack for three years before that, securing the land, and finally getting the cabin built. It was small, only two rooms, but the property was five acres and afforded me the privacy I wanted.

When I was back at the cabin and inside, I went into the bathroom, cranked the shower on, and got undressed. Once in the shower, I closed my eyes and braced a hand on the tile wall in front of me. My dick got hard pretty damn fast, and I didn't hesitate to grab hold of the thick length and give it a squeeze. My balls drew up tight, I clenched my jaw, and I started jerking off.

Moving my palm up and down my cock.

Stroking myself faster and harder.

Gritting my teeth.

I pictured a beautiful woman in front of me: nude, ready, and willing. I had a thing for red heads, so that's what I envisioned, with a thatch of trimmed red hair covering her cunt, she'd be so fucking eager for me.

"Fuck," I cursed as I came. I was like a damn teenager at how quickly I got off these days. It took nothing but a few pumps and squeezes on my cock before I exploded. I opened my eyes, seeing the last of my jizz coming out the tip of my shaft, the water washing it down the drain.

Shit.

I had to be a masochist to torture myself like this.

Was it really worth being alone and wanting my solitude if I had to resort to jerking myself off just so I didn't explode?

Vivian

I was sexually frustrated. I could admit that, own it even. But that didn't mean I liked being that way. It wasn't just about getting away for my own sanity, but also about the fact I wasn't getting what I wanted out of the relationships I've had.

Bland sex.

Vanilla touches.

No passion.

All of that and more summed up my past sexual relationships pretty damn well.

The truth was I was tired of city life, exhausted over the fact I couldn't find my niche in the world. I'd been doing the same thing for so long it was monotonous now.

I pulled her car up the gravel driveway of the cabin I'd rented for the week.

It was small, just one room that held the living room, kitchen, and bedroom. There was a small bathroom off the living room, and through the open doorway I saw a sink, toilet, and shower.

Damn, not even a tub.

I'd seen the pictures online, was glad it had been available on such a short, spur of the moment notice, and had hoped that in person it was still decent.

Getting out and grabbing my bag, I headed inside. The key was in a lockbox around the doorknob, and once I punched in the code and opened the door, I just stood there. It smelled like pine and vanilla and looked clean. I tossed my bag on the floor and went back to the car to grab the boxes of food and the case of water I'd picked up on my way up here.

Once back inside, I shut the door, turned the lights on, and looked around. It was quaint, homey even. It certainly wasn't what I was used to living in the city, and thank God for that.

I just stood there and listened.

There was nothing but stillness and the sound of my breathing.

Just silence.

I closed my eyes and just took it in, and for the first time in longer than I could even remember, I felt peace and calm.

Maybe I should have unpacked my shit, or just relaxed after the long drive, but instead, I put on my hiking boots, packed a small backpack with granola bars and two bottles of water, and decided to try out the trails that were right off the cabin property.

I stepped back outside, looked around, and just inhaled the clean, fresh air. I had lived in the city for so long, the smog and congestion had been my life, had been a part of me. I hadn't realized until this moment, when I was surrounded by the wilderness and the nothingness that I had been so trapped.

What a wonderful thought: just break away from it all, get my very own cabin, and move. But I didn't think I had the balls for all that. I might be a spur of the moment kind of girl, but that was jumping off a cliff without a parachute.

But, it was a thought, one that was plausible, and I knew living out here was something I definitely could get used to this.

Chapter Three

Vivian

I was lost, so fucking lost I didn't even know which direction I was anymore.

I stopped and turned in a circle, but everything looked exactly the same. I thought I'd stayed on the path, but part of it was overgrown, and before I knew what had happened, I was so far off where I'd started there was no way I could find my way back.

I lifted my hand and shielded my eyes from the setting sun. The light barely came through the branches above, and I knew if I didn't find shelter soon, I'd be staying the night in the woods.

And that was a big hell no on what I wanted to do, or how I wanted to spend my first night relaxing.

I started moving quicker, not sure if I was going North or South, or even toward town or the cabin.

I walked for another twenty minutes before I saw light breaking through the trees, and smelled the scent of smoke. Picking up my pace, and adjusting the straps on my backpack, I moved closer to the building.

A cabin.

I slowed until I came to a stop. The cabin was small, and I could see a light coming from the main window in front. I could see smoke coming from the chimney, and smelled it as if I stood right beside the fire.

I was in the middle of nowhere, or at least I thought I was. But someone clearly lived out here and was even home by the looks of it. I contemplated whether I should ask for help.

What if it's some maniac that chops up women and stores them in his cellar?

God, my imagination was having a field day right now.

Or maybe it's just someone that wants to be alone.

I heard the sound of wood being chopped, and glanced around, seeing if I could see who was wielding the ax. I could barely see a small shed on the other side of the cabin, and I mentally and physically forced myself to move closer.

What if there are women chained up in that shed?

Oh God, I was getting myself all worked up, picturing all those horror movies I'd watched back in the day featuring psychos and their harem of captives.

It was getting dark, and there was no way I wanted to stay in these woods when it was dark as hell.

Maybe I should have been even more frightened than I was, but I kept moving forward. I was exhausted, filthy, and even had leaves and pine needles in my hair. Every part of me hurt, and I realized just how out of shape I was. But I'd been walking aimlessly around the woods for hours, not even sure how far I was from my cabin or town.

The sound of wood being chopped suddenly stopped, and so did I. My heart was beating fast, and I adjusted the backpack I wore. I was out of water, only had one more granola bar left, and mosquitos were devouring me. Being inside sounded pretty damn good right now.

The sound of a door opening and closing rang out, echoing off the trees and making my pulse jump a bit. There was obviously a door in the back of the cabin since I still couldn't see anyone. And then I saw a massive shadow walk across the main window on the front of the cabin. There was a curtain covering the glass, but it was slightly sheer, and the shape—which had to belong to a man—looked huge.

Would I rather face what's in that cabin or what is roaming these woods at night?

Stealing myself and forcing my feet to start moving again, I kept a tight, almost painful hold on the straps of my backpack and took the porch steps one at a time. Once I was in front of the door, I held my breath, hearing my heart thundering.

Maybe a family lived here and I was just freaking myself out for nothing?

I heard the sound of twigs snapping in the distance, or maybe that was just my over reactive imagination? Either way I wasn't staying out here any longer. Without thinking about it anymore, I lifted my knuckles against on the door, and prayed whoever answered wasn't a psycho.

Jake

The sound of someone knocking on my door surprised me. I rarely got any visitors, and when I did, it was usually someone from work.

But that was rare.

I got off the couch, set my book on the coffee table, and walked toward the door. I took my ax off the hook by the door, and reached out for the handle. If it were someone who had no business being here, they'd find out pretty damn quickly what I could do with an ax.

I pulled the door open and immediately lowered my gaze to the disheveled as fuck woman standing on the other side. Maybe I was a sick fucking bastard, but my cock instantly got rock hard when I saw her.

She was gorgeous.

Her hair was a wreck, with debris from the woods stuck in the fire colored strands.

Red, my fucking favorite.

I realized neither of us had said anything for long moments, and I noticed her focus was on the ax I held.

"Um," she said in a low, very feminine voice.

I looked between her and my ax, and then set it aside.

"I'm out in the middle of nowhere. I don't get a lot of company," I said, explaining why I was holding an ax so she wouldn't be so freaked out. I didn't say anything after that, just waited to hear what she had to say, and why she was standing on my doorstep looking like she'd been rolling down a hill.

"I was hiking, but I'm lost," she finally said, licking her lips after the words were out.

She might be dirty as fuck from hiking, scared because she was lost and standing on a stranger's doorstep, but despite all of that, I was fucking rock hard for her. I was a bastard for the filthy images playing through my head, but I couldn't help my body's reaction to a gorgeous woman.

I hadn't been with a woman in five fucking years.

"Well, come in," I said and stepped aside. She was hesitant, and took a few seconds before she stepped over the threshold. I shut the door and looked her up and down. The jeans she wore formed to her tight ass, and I ran my hand over my cheeks, feeling the beard covering my flesh.

"Am I close to town?" she asked, her voice soft, tight. She turned around and faced me, and I stared into her light blue eyes.

"You're hours away from town." I heard her exhale, and I could see she was nervous and frustrated, as well as tired.

Just then the sound of thunder booming outside sounded.

"Of course it's about to storm," she said under her breath.

"You don't get out much, do you?" I asked in all seriousness.

She didn't answer me verbally, just shook he head.

"It storms often."

"I'm lost and in a strange man's house." She looked at me. "No offense. And it's about to storm."

"I'm Jake Braxton." I tried to keep my voice calm as I spoke, but my body wanted nothing more than to push everything aside and just take her right here. I wanted to hear her scream my name out as she came all over my cock.

I cleared my throat and got my thoughts in order. I certainly didn't want to come off as some asshole.

"I'm a lumberjack and have been living out here for the last five years." I told her the stats and saw the surprised look on her face. What exactly was she surprised about? Because I was an ax wielding man, who wore the stereotypical flannel shirts every day, and lived in the middle of nowhere?

"Now we aren't so much strangers anymore." I waited for her to give me something to go by, maybe even just her name, but she didn't say anything. She also looked tense as hell.

"You're a lumberjack? Seriously?"

I nodded.

She nodded. "Okay. I'm Vivian Clarke," she finally said, and started looking around the cabin again.

"Want a drink?" I asked.

She didn't answer right away, but did give me this 'are you fucking serious look'. I shrugged and went into the kitchen. "I figured after the day you've clearly had, you might want something to drink because you're either thirsty as fuck, or you need something stronger." I looked at her over my shoulder and saw she'd turned her head away from me quickly.

I couldn't help but feel this spark of lust slam into me at the thought that she might be staying the night due to the weather.

But I wasn't bringing that up right now, not when I'd just barely let her in the house, and she was clearly nervous.

The chances of me getting my dick wet in her sweet little body were pretty slim to none, but hell, I hadn't been this close to a woman in far too long.

"I have water ... or liquor. That's about it."

I checked her out a little more, and now that she wasn't looking, I adjusted my raging hard-on. Yeah, the fucker hadn't seen anything this sweet in a very long time. Finally, she turned back around and looked at the whiskey bottle I held.

"Liquor."

Yeah, I figured she'd need something a little harder after the night she was having.

Chapter Four

Vivian

I was in a strange man's cabin—a lumberjack of all things—and didn't know what in the hell to do. I didn't even know they actually called themselves lumberjacks, but it fit him pretty damn well.

I looked around again, seeing a big bed in one corner, a door that led to the bathroom across from that, and the large room that made up the kitchen and living room. Aside from a few pieces of furniture, the cabin was pretty sparse. There was a bookshelf, which was filled with books, though. Seeing as he didn't have a TV, I assumed that was how he spent his free time.

I took the glass from him and moved back a step. He went over to the fire and stoked it, and I couldn't help but stare at him.

He was huge, like the biggest man I'd ever seen. He had to be at least six and a half feet tall, and the muscles stacked upon muscles that covered his entire frame were a little intimidating. I didn't want to stare and seem creepy, but then again, he had to be used to it.

"What were you doing hiking all the way out here?" he asked without turning and facing me.

I didn't answer right away, mainly because I was too focused on the way the muscles on his back flexed as he pushed a piece of wood around. Embers seemed to float up from the flames, and when he finally faced me, I realized I still hadn't answered him.

"I'm staying in a cabin, and wanted to get out in the fresh air for a hike. I got lost." I turned and looked out the living window. "But I couldn't even tell you what direction my cabin's even in." I exhaled roughly.

He braced his arm on the mantle of the fireplace and just stared at me. He had shorter blond hair, and a full-on beard. With him living out here in the middle of nowhere, being as massive as he was, and clearly able to use an ax—and as a weapon when need be— I could image him as the perfect Mountain Man.

"You're from the city?"

I nodded, realizing I still hadn't had any of the whiskey. I ended up sucking the entire thing down in one go. It might only be a shot worth, but damn did it burn going down.

There was no expression on his face as I coughed and sputtered after swallowing the liquid fire, and I wondered if he saw me as some silly little girl that wanted to experience the wildlife.

As he watched me, he grabbed his glass off the mantle and downed the shot himself. He wore only a pair of jeans that were unbuttoned, the denim loose, yet they fit him pretty damn well. He had tattoos covering his arms and part of his chest, and although he had the Grizzly Adams thing going on, the ink looked good on him.

"How long have you been out here?" I asked, and he gestured for me to take a seat.

"Five years."

He left me in the living room, and I watched him go into the only other room in the house ... the bathroom. A second later he came out with a dark robe draped over his arm. He stopped a foot from me and held it out.

"What's this for?" I asked although I had a pretty good idea why he'd want me to put it on.

"Seeing as a storm is going to be rolling in, I figured you'd want to get cleaned up." He tipped his chin toward the bathroom. "There's a shower in that room."

I didn't speak for a second.

"The roads will get bogged down with mud from the weather, and there's no way you can get back to your cabin, or even town tonight."

I stared at him, not answering, because I knew what else he was going to say.

"You'll have to stay the night."

My heart thundered after he spoke.

"The robe is for after you shower, unless you want to wear your dirty clothes again?" He cocked an eyebrow.

I swallowed, my throat tight and dry. "And the roads will be too flooded to even attempt to go back to town, or to my cabin?" I asked, not even sure how to get back to my cabin from his place, even if he could have taken me back tonight.

He nodded.

I swallowed and thought about my options ... which were none as I wasn't prepared for what he said.

"Do you have a phone?" The look he gave me told me that was a big hell no. I didn't know whom I'd call anyway. If he couldn't get down the mountain, no one would be able to come up it.

"No landline and there isn't any cell service up here."

I stared into his green eyes.

"But I wouldn't have either anyway. I moved out here to get away from all that shit."

Of course he wouldn't have any form of communication living out here. My cabin was closer to town, and it had a landline, but his cabin was literally out in the middle of nowhere. I guess I'd had my hopes up that if it turned out he was a maniac, I'd have a way of contacting someone.

I had a cell phone, which was in my backpack, but it stopped working as soon as the mountains surrounded me.

"You're more than welcome to stay the night. The storm should pass by morning, and then I can take you into town, or back to wherever you're staying."

We stared at each other for long seconds.

"You normally just offer your house up to a strange woman?"

He crossed his big arms over his muscular chest and just looked at me. "I'm sure I'll be okay."

I couldn't help but check him out. I was a woman, and he was definitely all man.

"Or, you can brave the storm and the darkness, and try and find your way back." He was unmoving as he stood there.

"Maybe I'll be lucky and it'll pass."

"This storm has been coming since yesterday. It won't pass," he said with certainty.

He didn't look like he was concerned at whatever I decided to do.

I'd always had pretty good intuition when it came to these kinds of things, and I wasn't getting any fucked up signals from him. There was no fear or worry, and I relaxed a little more.

But then again I hadn't gotten any of those 'run and never look back' feelings when it came to that asshole Russ.

"Look, I'm not a psycho; I have no plans to keep you chained up in my cabin."

I had to snort at that, although maybe the smart thing to do would have been to be afraid he'd even said it out loud.

"I have food if you're hungry, something to drink if you're thirsty." He gestured to the liquor I held. "And I can give you shelter from the storm." He uncrossed his arms and ran a hand over his beard.

I'd never really found facial hair on a man attractive, maybe because I'd worked in corporate America for so long, but damn did his beard look good on him.

"You can take a shower and clean up, but if you plan on doing that you need to get it done before the storm comes."

I looked at the robe again, not sure how I felt about taking a shower in this stranger's house. But I also couldn't lie and say cleaning up, and the idea of hot water washing the day away, didn't sound like a very good idea.

"I don't care what you do either way, but I'm guessing the storm's gonna kick the power off, and after that you'll be shit out of luck."

And then he turned away and went back into the kitchen. I sat there for a moment contemplating what I should do, and after only a second, I just said fuck it.

"I'll be quick," I said, setting my glass down. I got up and headed to the bathroom. I figured if Jake was going to attack me, he could have done it already. Me cleaning up and trying to relax wouldn't change the situation, aside from making me feel a hell of a lot better.

Chapter Five

Jake

Hearing that damn shower kick on made me feel like Pavlov's dog. My already stiff cock seemed to get even harder. I reached down and adjusted the motherfucker, but even rubbing my hand over the denim-covered length had a guttural groan leaving me. I was doing my best to keep my shit under control, but it was hard with Vivian in my cabin where she would be staying the night.

I'd never been one to take something from a woman when she wasn't willing, and I wouldn't start now. But I also wasn't blind to the fact she had been eye fucking me since I opened the door. She hid it pretty well, maybe even a little better than I was, but I wasn't blind.

I felt drawn to her, and I couldn't really understand why. But I also wasn't about to question it too hard. In the last five years I'd had sexual desires, obviously, but hadn't wanted to go into town to get a piece. I'd just built this wall around myself, because even if my ex hadn't been the woman I'd seen myself marrying and having a family with, she'd still fucked things up for me in that department. The betrayal had been really fucked up.

But, at thirty-five I wasn't getting any younger, and having Vivian here really made me think how long I'd isolated myself.

If it came down to it and she was ready to get this on, I was more than willing to give her a night she wouldn't forget.

I braced my hands on the edge of the sink and looked out the window. The sun was almost fully set, but even with the little bit of light in the sky, I could see the angry clouds rolling in. Yeah, I'd heard about this storm coming since yesterday, had even made a special trek down the mountain and into town to grab provisions. This was going to be a bad one, but it looked like I wouldn't be spending it alone.

Hell, even if I didn't get to sample the little redhead, having her in the cabin, and the sweet scent that seemed to surround her, was pretty damn nice. It made me realize how much I fucking missed a woman.

Or maybe it's Vivian that has me feeling that?

After I'd made her a sandwich, just in case she was hungry, I heard the shower turn off. I clenched my hands at my sides and couldn't help but envision her stepping out of the shower naked, water dripping off her body. Even through her clothes, I'd been able to tell she was curvy in all the right places. Was she a natural redhead? Fuck, just thinking that she was, and that her pussy hair was the same intense red as the long waves that covered her head, had me unable to hold back a groan.

I grabbed a bottle of water and the plate with the sandwich on it and headed to the living room. Setting the items on the coffee table, I ran my palms over my thighs and stared at the fire. I was antsy to see her again, and that should have had this awkwardness filling me. But the truth was no one, not even when I'd lived in the city, had ever made me feel like this. I could blame it on basically being celibate for so long, but I liked looking at her, hearing her voice, and seeing her reaction to comments I made.

The sound of the fire crackling didn't stop the hum of lust moving through me. I grabbed a few more logs and put them in the fireplace, stoking it with a poker. I was trying to keep myself busy and my mind off shit that I shouldn't even be thinking about.

And then the bathroom door opened, and I couldn't help but look.

Vivian had my robe wrapped tightly around her, the material so oversized I couldn't help thinking she looked cute in it. She had her hand up by her neck, clutching at the lapels and looking nervous.

Moving over to the chair and sitting down by the fire, I gestured to the plate and water. "If you're hungry." I kept my head slightly lowered as I watched her approach.

She sat down across from me, grabbed the plate, and eyed it a little. "Thanks ... for everything." Vivian lifted her head and our eyes connected.

I could have said it was no trouble and I'd do this for anyone, but that would have been a lie. If some asshole had come out here looking for a place to crash, I would have sent him on his way. I wasn't a prick; I just liked my privacy.

But then I'd seen Vivian standing on my doorstep, and I'd wanted nothing more than to bring her inside and make her mine. The attraction had been instant and consuming.

"You're welcome," I finally said after long seconds of silence. I didn't stay sitting, though, and instead got up and grabbed candles. I knew the power would go out sooner rather than later.

Fuck! Being alone with her with the power off, the only light coming from the fire and the candles ... yeah, the very image almost had me coming right in my fucking jeans.

Vivian

We'd been sitting here for over an hour. I'd finished the sandwich and bottle of water Jake had given me, and I was trying desperately not to reveal my desires. We really hadn't been talking; after I'd finished eating, I'd helped myself to one of the many books on his shelves. But I wasn't reading the damn thing. I couldn't help but watch what Jake was doing this whole time.

Candles had been lit just in time as the lights began to flicker off and on, and then finally off for good. The thunder and lightening was fierce, and the rain pelted the windows.

Jake now sat across from me, cleaning and sharpening the blade of his ax. Maybe doing that should have scared me, because it was intimidating watching him do it, but I wasn't afraid of him.

I was wet for him.

Watching Jake run the cloth over the metal, following the sharp end of the blade as he sharpened it ... all of that had my body so coiled I knew if I'd gone into the bathroom and touched my clit, I'd come in seconds.

Jake set the cloth down, got up, and put his ax back up on the hook on the wall. Never in my life would I have thought a lumberjack could be so damn sexy.

I was aroused, so damn wet I couldn't even think straight. I'd never been this turned on, and nothing sexual had even happened. Was I so sexually repressed that some alcohol, the ambience of no electricity, a roaring fire, and a lumberjack—literally—of a man, had me so turned on I couldn't even think rationally?

Did I even want to think rationally? Did I want to just "play it safe"?

"Do you want more?" he asked in that gruff, deep voice of his, gesturing toward my empty whiskey glass.

I nodded, because right now a little more liquid courage would definitely help ease my nerves and my heightened arousal.

I watched as Jake walked into the kitchen. The cabin was small, but definitely comfortable. It suited him, although I had no idea who he was as a person. But just looking at him, knowing the small fact that he was here and was a lumberjack, I thought this space fit him well.

He had his back to me as he poured us more whiskey, and I took the time to stare at the muscle definition of his body. I wasn't blind to the raw power he exuded. He was all man, through and through, and I felt like a girl in heat at how much I wanted him.

And then he turned and faced me, the two glasses in his hands now filled with the amber colored liquid. I let my gaze travel over the lines and dips, the hollows and ridges of his chest. His pectoral muscles were shaped, and the six-pack lining his abdomen, and the V of muscle that disappeared beneath his jeans had my inner muscles clenching.

Just looking at him and I felt like I hadn't been with a man in years, like I'd never been properly fucked. But hell, I just *knew* Jake could more than handle that job. The images in my head were pretty dirty, certainly not ladylike, but I didn't care. I wanted him, and the alcohol I'd consumed was helping my inhibitions diminish every single second.

The electricity was off, and the only light came from the fire and the few candles placed around the room. The alcohol flowed through my veins, and the sight and scent of Jake—male in all sense of the word—I just wanted to let loose and say fuck everything else. I'd never had one-night stand, and that's all being with Jake would ever be, but the very thought of just giving into my basic urges was so very appealing.

He handed me the glass and sat back down. I greedily drank it while I stared at him. I'd only been here for a few hours, and already I felt like tearing off this robe and just presenting myself to him in the most erotic, obscene gesture imaginable.

God, I am being so insane right now.

He hadn't taken a drink yet; instead, he watched me act like a lush.

"I don't usually drink this much."

It was the truth, and I guess my arousal was so intense it was clouding my brain.

"So you've been out here alone for that long?" I asked although he'd already told me as much. I took another drink and watched him lean back on the chair. His chest clenched from the movement, and my mouth watered as I tried not to look like a creep because I wanted him really badly.

"Yes," he said and took a drink of his whiskey.

"And you've been alone this whole time?"

He took another drink, moved the glass away, and balanced the glass on his knee. "Yeah."

I nodded and looked down at his feet. They were bare, and I noticed even they were attractive.

"And you chop wood for a living?" Obviously he did, but I was nervous rambling now.

"To break it down to its simplest form, yeah, I chop wood for a living." He smirked, just the corner of his mouth lifting up, and I felt my entire body heat.

I looked over at the ax he had on the wall. It was huge, the handle worn, but the blade freshly cleaned and sharpened. I imagined the kind of power it must take to wield that thing day in and day out.

When I turned my head to face him again, I was surprised to see he was leaning forward, his focus on me. He was braced on the edge of the chair, his glass now on the coffee table, and his forearms resting on his thighs. He kept his focus right on my eyes, and I felt my heart jump into my throat.

"How about we cut the shit, Vivian?"

The way he spoke, the words he said, were heated, aroused.

I clenched my fingers tighter around my glass.

Was the room getting hotter, or was it just me?

"What?" I said softly. "What are you talking about?" God, even hearing myself, I sounded like I was full of shit.

He lifted his eyebrow at my question, but didn't respond right away. After another moment of silence, he finally spoke again. "You want to act like you're not aroused right now, that you don't feel this crazy as fuck chemistry?"

I swallowed, not saying anything, but knowing my answer was probably written all over my face.

"You want to pretend like you're not eyeing every part of my body, maybe wondering how big my cock is?"

Oh. God.

"Because I sure as fuck have been eyeing you, wondering if your pussy hair matches what's on your head."

The deep sound of his voice had my inner muscles clenching even tighter in desire.

His eyes were half lidded as he stared at me. "Because I'll tell you one thing." A moment passed before he continued. "Red is my favorite fucking color."

I think my ovaries just exploded.

Of course, I'd wondered if the bulge I'd seen him sporting was just as impressive in the flesh.

"I haven't been with a woman in five fucking years, Vivian."

I felt my eyes widen. And then he stood, and all I could do was sit there and watch him come closer. He took the glass out of my hand and set it beside him on the table. But he didn't move after that, just stood in front of me, his jean-covered dick right in my face, his erection tenting the material.

"Admit you want me as much as I want you."

I lifted my eyes from his bulge to his face. His eyes were half-lidded, his lips just barely parted.

"Go on," he coaxed, challenged. "Tell me."

Could I do this? Admit I wanted a man I'd just met a few hours ago? The storm waged on outside, and the whole ambience of the night had me feeling far more intoxicated than I probably was. But I was going to say those words. Since coming out to the wilderness I had never felt freer. And shouldn't I live my life the way I want, even if that meant sleeping with this burly lumberjack of a man?

"Yes," I whispered. "I want you."

There was no going back now.

Not that I wanted to.

Chapter Six

Jake

I had Vivian off the couch in a matter of seconds. She'd told me she wanted this; she wanted me, and I was about to give it to her. I pressed my body to hers, dug my hard cock into her belly, and couldn't hold back the gruff sound that came from me.

"I don't know if you realize what you've agreed to," I said on a growl and looked at her lips. "Five years without a woman has made me feral, Vivian." I lifted my gaze and looked at her eyes. "And once we start, we won't be stopping until you've come on my cock more than once."

She parted her lips and sucked in a breath.

"I'm going to fuck you so good and raw, you won't be able to sit comfortably tomorrow without thinking of my cock all up in you."

"God," she whispered.

"I'll have you screaming more than that by the time we're done." I felt like this beast had broken free inside of me, like I couldn't control myself. I wanted her so damn badly, and although I had a lot of pent-up desires, I knew I wouldn't have been this frenzied with just any woman.

Something about Vivian drove me to the brink of coming right in my jeans. Seeing her standing on my doorstep, her red hair mussed, her body so feminine, so much smaller than mine had appealed to me.

Yeah, I'd wanted to mount her right then and there.

I grabbed a chunk of her damp red hair, pulled her head back so her throat was bared, and leaned down to run my tongue up and down the arch. God, she tasted fucking incredible, fresh and clean, like lemons. And she smelled like me. It had this possessive side rising up in me.

"I'm about to claim every single part of you." I stared right into her eyes. "I'm about to own every inch of you." I lowered my voice. "And when I'm done with you, Vivian, you'll know exactly what it's like to be with a real man."

And when it's all said and done, I don't know if I'll be able to let you walk away.

Vivian

His mouth was on mine a second later. I melted against him, never having felt this type of masculinity before. His cock dug into my belly, hard, thick, huge. I most certainly had never been with a man this big ... all over.

He still had his hand in my hair, his fingers tangled in the strands. He used his other hand to snake down my back to cup my ass through the robe.

I wanted the damn thing off.

He kissed me raw and hard, sweeping his tongue inside of my mouth and claiming me fully. I'd never felt so possessed by a man before. The hand in my hair tightened, sending a sting of pleasurable pain through my scalp, to my breasts, and finally straight to the center of my pussy.

I moaned, and it was as if that sound triggered something else in him. Jake gripped my waist with both hands and lifted me off the ground effortlessly. I imagined him wielding that ax, using all the strength every single day. My pussy clenched and became wetter.

I tightened my legs around his waist. The robe parted, and I was nude under the material. I felt the warm, hard skin of his abdomen right on my pussy. A gasp left me at how sensitive I was.

He grunted, held me up with one arm, and gripped the back of my hair again with his other hand. With my throat arched once more, he broke the kiss and dragged his tongue up my neck. God, I was falling in love with that act. It had my entire body tingling.

And then he set me on the ground, took a step back, and, in one swift move, removed the robe from me.

There I stood, stark naked, my nipples hard, my breasts feeling full, and my pussy so wet I wouldn't have been surprised if some of that cream trailed down my inner thigh.

He looked his fill, and I shivered in response, not even able to stop myself from reacting. Jake moved closer, slipped his hand under over the curve of my ass while holding his gaze with mine, and squeezed the flesh. I felt every callus along the pads of his fingers. It was a testament to the manual labor he did.

"Are you wet for me?" he asked in a low voice.

I could only nod.

"You want me to touch your wet pussy?"

Again, I could only nod.

He ran his teeth up and down my neck, nipped at my flesh, and thrust his erection against my belly. I couldn't handle all this hotness, all this maleness personified. I was going to die if I didn't feel him in me, making me forget about every shitty thing that I'd ever dealt with.

I was feverish and excited; all I could think about was how it would feel to have him thrust all those thick inches into me.

"Fuck, I'm so damn hard for you I can't stand it."

My body tingled even more after he spoke.

He murmured something low and gruff against my temple, and I closed my eyes and just absorbed it all. I felt like a damn virgin at how aroused this man made me feel. I'd never felt this kind of intensity before.

Moving my hands between our bodies, I fumbled for the zipper of his jeans. I needed them off, needed to see what he was working with. Apparently, he wasn't having any of that, because, in the next second, he had his hands around my waist again and had me turned over the back of the couch.

I clenched my fingers in the fabric and looked over my shoulder at him.

The look on his face had this small sound escaping me. I felt my eyes widen when he crouched on his haunches right behind me, the feel of his warm, humid breath moving along the cheeks of my ass.

I was hyperventilating at this point.

He groaned and palmed my ass right before he ran his nose up and down the crease of my bottom. "You smell so fucking good." The heavy weight of his palm landed on my right ass cheek, and a squeak of pleasure and surprise slipped out. He lifted his gaze and stared right at me. "You like when I do that?"

I nodded. Yeah, I really did.

While still staring at me, he brought his hand down on the other ass cheek. Jake did this over and over again, alternating between both mounds until they felt hot, but in a good way.

"Fuck, you have a perfect ass, big, juicy, and so damn fuckable."

Fuckable?

I'd never had anal before, but to be honest, right now, I'd let Jake do anything he wanted.

He curled his fingers into the skin of my ass and started moving the flesh back and forth, causing the mounds to shake. I bit my lip and closed my eyes as ecstasy stole over me. The air left me, and I snapped my eyes open when he spread my ass wide open.

"Yeah, so fuckable." And then he ran his tongue up and down the slit of my pussy. He sucked and licked, nipped and hummed along my swollen, heated flesh. "It's been so long, Vivian," he murmured against my flesh.

He was relentless in his onslaught, and I didn't want him to stop.

I was either far more repressed than I thought, or Jake knew exactly how to press my buttons to get me off.

I was going to come.

But, of course, just as I was about to get off—for the first time in months—he moved away. I groaned in frustration and heard him chuckle behind me. He gave my ass a smack, pulled the cheeks apart again, and went back to eating me out.

"You won't come until I say you can," he said against my flesh, his words muffled. He ran his tongue along the cleft of my pussy, and kept going until he was licking my asshole. I curled my fingers into the couch even more. It was an unusual feeling to have someone licking me back there, but it also felt really damn good.

He groaned against my flesh as he licked at me, his hands on my ass, his fingers digging painfully into my skin. But I loved that discomfort.

"God, you smell so damn good." Over and over, he massaged the globes of my ass, pulling the cheeks apart even wider, but then letting them fall back into place and frame his face. It was erotic, hot, and kind of taboo to have him eating out my ass.

But I wanted more, so much more.

I was close to coming, even if he wasn't touching my pussy, but I held off. I forced myself to maintain a small amount of self-control.

"Ask me for it, baby," Jake said and brought his hand down on one of my ass cheeks hard.

"God," I moaned.

He slapped the cheek again, obviously wanting me to beg for it.

I was not above doing just that.

"If you want my cock in your cunt, you'll ask me for it."

Oh. God.

"And I know you want all ten inches of my huge cock shoved deep inside of you."

Ten inches?

Shit.

His words were so vulgar. Goddammit, they turned me on.

"Give it to me," I said with more force than I thought I could have mustered right then. "Give me that big cock."

He groaned and smacked my ass; at the same time he ran his tongue along my asshole.

"You smell like me, like my soap." He tightened his hold on my flesh, his beard moving along my flesh. "That's so fucking hot." With one more lick up the crack of my ass, Jake moved away. I looked over my shoulder and watched him as he stood behind me, his focus on my pussy and bottom, his cock looking huge behind his fly.

Sucking in a lungful of air, I felt my body tighten further when he started taking off his jeans. He was huge and hard ... everywhere. I'd always gone for the "pretty boys", but Jake definitely didn't fit in that category. He was rugged and rough around the edges, with short darker blond hair covering his pectoral muscles, and a line of it going right down to the monster between his legs.

His dick was, without a doubt, the biggest one I'd ever seen.

Taking hold of the root of his cock, he stroked it a few times while he looked me right in the eyes.

"Reach behind and spread your ass for me." His words were a command, an order.

I was not about to disobey him.

I grabbed each cheek and pulled them apart, showing him how wet I was for him, how primed I was for his cock.

"Motherfucker, I can't get over how pink and wet you are for me."

I was soaked for Jake.

He stepped closer and ran his finger down my pussy slit. He stopped when he reached my hole, and while still focused on my eyes, he shoved that thick finger right into my cunt. Immediately, my muscles clamped down on the digit. It felt good, but I needed something much bigger.

He grunted in approval.

"I'm going to have my dick in here, Vivian," he said and started pumping that thick finger in me. "I'm going to fill you with my cum, make you mine."

I couldn't help the sound that left me.

He pulled his finger out and immediately lifted it to his mouth to suck the glossiness from it. "Mmmm. You taste so damn good." And then he was behind me, holding onto my hip with one hand, and aligning the tip of his dick with the other.

A groan spilled out of me at the sensation of his thick cockhead right at my pussy hole.

"I need it raw, Vivian. I need to feel your pussy walls around me. I don't want anything between us." We looked at each for a second. "I don't have a condom anyway, but I'm clean."

I swallowed, because I'd been so aroused I hadn't even thought about protection. I was on the pill anyway, so pregnancy wise we were good. If I was doing this, then I was *really* doing it. "Fuck me, Jake."

"Fucking demanding, baby." He dug his fingers into my hips, and I knew there would be bruises come morning.

Good. It made me wetter, knowing I'd have his brand of ownership on my body.

He used his foot to kick my feet apart even more, and then he was pushing into me with a slow but very thorough thrust.

"Don't go slow," I moaned in frustration. "Just shove that big dick in me."

His expression heated further; he let out this low sound, and then he was shoving all ten inches into me in a forceful thrust. I was filled completely, stretched to the point it felt like I'd split in two, but Goddamn, did it feel good.

"You might have been with men that like you to be in control," he said and spanked my ass especially hard. "But here, with me, I'm the one in control." He pulled out so just the tip was lodged in me. "With me, Vivian, I'm the man, and you're the woman."

The way he said that had me feeling like he'd show me exactly how manly he could be.

"When you're with me, I'm the one that does the fucking, baby, not the other way around."

All I could do was nod in agreement and understanding.

Jake started fucking me then. Pulling out and shoving all this thick inches back into me. My inner muscles clenched around his length, and he grunted, picking up his speed and intensity.

"I want this to last, but you feel too good," he groaned the words out.

I rested my forehead on the back of the couch, just holding on as he fucked the hell out of me. He certainly showed me what it was like to be with a real man.

He let go of my waist and spread my ass cheeks so wide I knew he was watching his cock move in and out of me.

"Fucking hell, baby." He picked up speed and slammed harder into me. "Your cunt is so fucking tight and wet." He groaned.

"You're so damn hot." He thrust into me again and again until I couldn't see straight.

"I'm going to come." I didn't want this to end, but I also wanted to just let go.

"Not yet," he said and leaned forward to run his tongue up the length of my spine. "Even your sweat is so damn sweet." He worked his dick inside of me in deep, long strokes, and I curled my hands into the couch until I felt pain take root in my knuckles.

Droplets of Jake's sweat landed on my back, and I arched up. Maybe it was animalistic of me, but I wanted his perspiration covering me, marking me.

He continued to thrust into me, and I forced myself to hold off on coming because of his command, but I was doing shitty job of it. I bit my lip, tasting blood, and realized I'd broken the skin. He pumped three more times into me before stilling, his balls pressed against my pussy.

"You want to come?"

I nodded, not able to form a coherent word.

He pulled out so the tip was at my entrance again. "Then come all over my cock. Soak me in it." And he thrust back in so powerfully I did come for him.

Lights flashed in front of my eyes, my head felt fuzzy, and it was as if the world swallowed me whole. The pleasure was like nothing I'd ever felt before, and the fact Jake kept fucking me only made it that much better. Right before the high left me, Jake pulled out and turned me around. He had me in his arms a second later. I wrapped my legs around his waist, feeling his wet cock tease my folds, my eyes pleading for more.

Jake reached between us, placed his cock back at my entrance, and shoved into me hard. I cried out and closed my eyes. I was holding onto him with my legs around his waist and my arms around his neck. But he was so strong. I knew *he* was the one doing all the holding.

He started moving toward the bed, his cock still in me, his mouth now at my neck. He ran his teeth up and down the side of my throat, and I exhaled. That one orgasm hadn't done anything to dim the arousal in me.

"I hope you've got the stamina to keep going, baby, because I'm not done with you yet."

He pulled out of me. And before I knew what was happening, or could demand he continue fucking me, Jake all but threw me onto the center of his bed. The scent of him washed over me. It was concentrated, wild, and woodsy. Before I could even prepare myself for what he was about to do, Jake was on top of me, his big body pressing me into the mattress. He gripped my thighs, pulled them open, and had his dick back in me all in a matter of seconds.

I opened my mouth on a silent cry at the feeling of being so filled and stretched. My pussy was tender, but it was the kind of discomfort that turned me on.

He was breathing hard now, his massive chest rising and falling. "I am going to tear you up, Vivian, devour every fucking inch of you." He certainly had showed me exactly what he was made of. He started thrusting into me shallowly. "Tomorrow, you will still feel my big dick in your pussy and will remember everything I have done to you."

"Yes," I found myself whispering.

"*Christ.*"

His voice was so rough it was like sandpaper moving all over my body. The corded muscles and tendons that were laced and bulging under his skin made me feel so feminine. The thick crest of his cock pressed against my pussy hole again, and he paused for a second. Maybe he wanted to torment me, or maybe he was grappling with his own control. And then he started fucking me with frenzied movements.

My body slid up the bed, my head hitting the headboard. I gasped at how forceful his thrusts were, but I dug my nails into his flesh, wanting more.

"Look at me." Jake's voice was deep and commanding. It was like everything around me faded until there was only this one moment in time. He was braced above me, his arms locked, his muscles straining. "I want you to watch while I slam my cock into your tight little cunt." He looked at my mouth. "I want you to watch as I make you mine."

I knew it was the 'heat of the moment' kind of thing; it's why he'd said all these possessive things, but hell, I wanted to hear more.

There had never been a time when I had felt this kind of chemistry or arousal. I'd never wanted someone as much as I wanted Jake. I didn't know if that should frighten or excite me. I lifted up and braced myself on my elbows, my focus down the length of my body. I'd never watched a man fuck me. I just let it happen and hoped I got off.

But with Jake the entire experience was so different ... so fucking incredible.

He slowly pulled out of me, and I watched his cock become visible, my cream coating the thickness. Jake pushed it back into me, and it took all my strength to hold myself up and watch.

"Isn't it so fucking hot, baby?"

I could only nod.

Arms shaking and breath leaving me in uneven gasps, I knew I couldn't hold out much longer. I didn't want to, even if Jake hadn't told me I could come.

Chapter Seven

Jake

I should have gotten a fucking medal for how much self-control I was showing with Vivian.

I watched my dick slide in and out of her tight cunt. Her flesh was pink, wet, and swollen; it gripped me like an iron-fist. I'd never felt anything so good, never needed to fuck a woman this badly.

I had a tight grip on her outer thighs and curled my fingers even harder into her flesh. I wanted my mark on her, wanted her creamy flesh painted blue, showing her my ownership.

And I *was* owning her ... every part.

The slickness of her pussy and the suctioning warmth that surrounded my cock had my orgasm rushing close to the surface. I didn't want it to end. Especially when I had never felt anything as good as Vivian. But I had to give in eventually. She had to be sore from me fucking the hell out of her.

"Yeah, baby. You feel so fucking good." I pushed into her and pulled back out. I did this over and over again, picking up my speed until my balls slapped her ass and sweat beaded my body. My focus was trained on her tits, which bounced back and forth. They were huge. I leaned forward and ran my tongue along one stiff nipple. The peak was hard, elongated, and I gently bit it.

It had been a while since I'd had a woman, so of course, the thought that maybe that's where all this possessiveness was coming from filled my head. But as soon as I thought of it, I pushed it away.

Vivian was different. She'd lived the same life I had, known the suffocating feeling of being trapped in a life that wasn't going anywhere.

We might have only known each other for a few hours, but there was no way I could let her walk away. This was fast, frantic, and maybe it didn't make much sense, but I was going with my gut on this.

I wanted Vivian as mine.

She lifted her hands and ran her fingers through my chest hair. I knew she was going to come again. Her eyes were glazed over, her mouth parted, and her cheeks pink. Her moans were soft and needy, and I worked my hips against her with a little more power. Thrusting as hard and fast as I was caused the large globes to bounce up and down even harder.

It was obscene.

It was fucking hot.

"I need you to come for me again. I need to see you let go before I can." I lowered my gaze to her pussy and watched my cock tunnel in and out of her. "Pull your pussy lips apart. Let me see all that pink, wet perfection."

She rested back on the bed and did what I told her. My cock stretched her wide. The sight of her flesh pulled apart transfixed me. And then she squeezed her pussy around my cock.

"That's it, baby. Milk my fucking cock. Get all that cum from me." I reached down and started rubbing her engorged clit back and forth. "Come for me, Vivian." I looked into her eyes while fucking her pussy and rubbing her clit. "One more time, baby. Just give me one more."

And she did just that, obeying me like a good girl.

I watched her face shift from arousal to ecstasy as she got off, and I felt my own orgasm rise up. I wasn't going to be able to stop it this time.

Once, twice, and on the third thrust, I buried my cock as far inside her as I could. I came long and hard, filling her body with my spunk, making her take every last drop. My body was tense, my muscles strained. Fuck, I couldn't even keep my eyes open because of how good it felt.

"Fuck. Yes." The words just spilled from me, but I didn't care. "You're mine." Vivian needed to know what she did to me, how I saw her.

I collapsed on top of her; my balls drained dry, my heart thundering in my chest. I quickly rolled away so I didn't crush her, but I wanted her right up against me. I pulled her in right up next to my body, placed my hand between her thighs, right over her hot, wet cunt, and kissed the top of her head.

"Get some sleep, baby."

I got pissed even thinking about her leaving. I didn't know if I could do it, because I'd had her, and I wanted more ... so much more. I realized I was a possessive bastard when it came to Vivian.

Chapter Eight

Vivian

The sound of wood being chopped and the smell of coffee woke me. I lay still, staring at the exposed beam ceiling above me, and listening to the sounds of wood splintering. Lifting my arms above my head, I stretched, feeling deliciously sore all over.

Jake had worked me over in ways I hadn't even known possible.

My ass, pussy, and even my tits were sore from his hands, mouth, and cock. He'd used up all that pent-up arousal that had been brewing all these years out here alone, and he made sure I knew exactly what it felt like to be thoroughly fucked by a man.

I could honestly say I'd never had a man be that way with me, act so primal and intense. The guys I'd been with now looked like dead fish between the sheets compared to Jake.

Forcing myself out of bed, I sat on the edge of the mattress for a second as my muscles protested. I was sore as hell between my thighs, and the memories of why I was so sore played through my head. My inner muscles clenched, and I became warm all over. When I finally forced myself to stand, my knees shook.

Damn, I'd be walking bowlegged for sure.

I searched for the robe from last night, but then I remembered it was probably still on the living room floor. But just as I was about to get up and grab the robe, I saw a t-shirt and pair of sweats sitting on the dresser. I didn't know if he'd left them there for me, but I was wearing them.

Once I was dressed, I looked down at myself. The fabric hung on me. Obviously Jake's clothes, I swam in them. The scent of him invaded my head, and I got this rush of desire. It wasn't cologne that came through, but this woodsy, manly scent. My Mountain Man certainly had it going on in all departments.

My *Mountain Man?*

Had I already claimed him after one night? I reminded myself I had a life back in the city, and once this week was up, I'd have to leave all of this—Jake included—behind. I didn't know why that bothered me as much as it did. The very thought of leaving all of this behind: a man that had opened my eyes to mind blowing pleasure and to a kind of freedom I'd never experienced before, really bothered me.

I went over to the window and pulled the curtain aside, but the angle of the window didn't allow me to see Jake doing his lumberjack thing. Leaving the room and making my way into the kitchen, the sight of the full coffee pot had me perking up right away. After grabbing a coffee mug and filling it up, I drank the steaming liquid while staring out the window above the sink. I normally drank my coffee with milk and sugar, but after last night, I needed something pretty damn strong to wake me up.

I finally made my way toward the back door, opened it, and stepped out onto the small deck. And that's when I saw him.

He had on boots, a pair of well-worn jeans, and a white t-shirt. But the shirt was soaked with sweat, and the sight of his muscles clearly visible through the damp material had me getting all kinds of hot and bothered. I leaned against the railing, holding the cup between my hands, and getting a nice eyeful of how hot it was to see Jake doing manual labor.

He lifted the ax above his head, and it was like slow motion as I watched his biceps flex with power. He brought that weapon down on the wood, splitting it in two, and instantly grabbing another log. Once it on the chopping block, he repeated the action.

He did this for a few more minutes before setting his ax against the block and removing his shirt.

Well, shit, it was like my very own porn movie. He reached behind his head and grabbed a chunk of the material before lifting it up and over his head. Once the shirt was off, he wiped his face with the fabric, his back muscles contracting and relaxing from the act. He tossed the t-shirt aside and went back to work.

He either didn't know I was watching him like a horny sorority girl, or he liked the audience. Either way, I wasn't about to break his concentration by letting my presence be known.

Beads of sweat trailed down the length of his spine, and I clenched my thighs together. Hell, you wouldn't know I had just been thoroughly fucked last night based on how aroused I was at watching him.

Jake took the term lumberjack to a whole new level.

I don't know how long I watched him, but by the time he cut the last log and tossed the pieces onto the woodpile, I was soaked between my thighs, and my nipples were stabbing through the material of my shirt.

Jake turned around then, our eyes locked, and I swear I could feel his arousal slam right into me. Neither of us moved for long seconds, and I forced myself to stand straight, set my coffee sup on the railing, and take in a steadying breath. He looked down at my chest; there was no doubt in my mind he could see how hard my nipples were.

The sound that left him seemed pretty damn animalistic, and it thrilled me. And then I saw something shift in his gaze right before he stalked forward like he was ready to mount me.

God, I hoped he was about to mount me.

Jake

I could blame my insatiable sexual appetite on the fact I'd been dry in that department for years, but the truth was there was something about Vivian that had all of my self control snapping right in two.

We'd fucked so hard and fierce last night that I was surprised that I could even get hard, but the fucker between my legs was standing at attention. When I saw she'd been watching me cut wood, staring at me like she was picturing me naked, all I could think about was bending her over the deck railing and fucking the hell out of her.

And I planned on doing just that.

Pleasantries and me being a gentleman could happen when I'd sated both of our needs. And I knew she wanted my dick all up in her, because the look she gave me screamed 'fuck me now'."

I wanted my hands on her bare ass, wanted my cock buried deep in her pussy, and I was going after that right now.

I was on the deck in seconds flat, stopped right in front of her, and growled low at how good she looked in my clothes. But I need them off her now.

"You look positively wild," she breathed out.

That's exactly how I felt when I looked at her.

"Strip for me," I ordered.

She shivered visibly, but obeyed right away. I made a low sound in my throat at how much that pleased me. I wasn't going to last long, but right now wasn't about stamina, but about both of us getting off.

She had the shirt and sweats off in seconds, and for long moments I looked my fucking fill of her. Her tits were big, her nipples a dusky rose color. Her long red hair hung in waves over her shoulders, and her trimmed pussy hair, which was the same shade as the strands on her head, had my cock jerking.

"Red is my fucking favorite color."

She gasped, but didn't answer. I knew I'd told her that already, but I didn't care if I had. I wanted her to know again.

I unbuttoned my jeans, pulled the zipper down, and grabbed my cock. I gave the fucker a few strokes, pre-cum coming out of the slit, and my whole body tensed, that's how ready I was for her. She watched me jerk off.

"You like this?" I asked and held my dick in my hand, pointing the length right at her.

She nodded.

"Turn around," I ordered, and when she was in position, I stepped up behind her. Grabbing her right ass cheek, I shook the flesh. I brought my hand down on the mound, hearing flesh hitting flesh, and growling out. I swatted her ass again, and on the third time, I watched as her flesh turned pink.

Vivian looked over her shoulder at me. "Are you going to fuck me, or what?"

She wanted me to fuck her? Oh, I'd fuck her raw.

I placed my hand on her lower back and slid it up her spine. Once I reached the center, I pushed her forward. She was bent over the banister now, her tits hanging freely over the wood, and her legs spread wide. I leaned back enough to look at her pussy on display for me; I couldn't wait to give her exactly what she wanted.

I grabbed my cock, placed it at her entrance, and in one big thrust, I buried all of it in her cunt. We both groaned; I closed my eyes and gripped her hips. My dick throbbed in her, and the feel of her inner muscles clenching around my shaft had me nearly filling her up right then and there.

She gripped the banister and moaned.

Yeah, I'd give it to her all right; give it to her until she screamed my name over and over again. She'd go back to the city and think about me every time she wanted some cock.

The very thought of her leaving, of another man touching her, had me so fucking pissed I saw red.

She was mine. Her pussy, tits, ass ... every part of her was mine.

"You're mine," I found myself saying before I could stop the words from spilling out. Hell, we'd known each other less than a full day, and here I was getting all possessive and shit. But I wouldn't take it back, and after our time together was done, she'd know what it meant to be owned.

I started pounding in and out of her, faster and harder, trying to get as deep as I could.

"Jake," she moaned.

Yeah, I fucking loved hearing her say my name when I had my cock deep in her body. Her ass shook from how forceful my thrusts were, but we were both moaning, and I knew she loved it.

"God, yes," she cried out and threw her head back. I reached up and grabbed a chunk of her hair, keeping her throat arched as I thrust in and out of her. Fuck, the sounds she made had my balls drawing up tight. I didn't want to come yet, not until she did, not until she knew she belonged to me. But, shit, I was so damn close already.

I was already sweaty from chopping wood, but more beads started to form on my face and chest as I worked my dick in and out of her.

"I'm coming," she whispered, her mouth parted, her eyes closed.

Thank fuck, because I was having a hell of a time holding onto my control.

I pulled back, watched my cock sink in and out of her, saw the way her cunt cream glistened on my shaft, and everything went hazy. And when I felt her pussy muscles contract especially hard around my dick, I couldn't stop myself from coming.

I buried myself all the way inside her, had my hand on the center of her back, keeping her in the position I wanted, and filled her body with my cum. I groaned out once more as the last of my jizz shot deep inside her. When I was milked dry, I pulled out and looked down at her pussy. Grabbing her ass cheeks and spreading them wider, I saw my cum slide out of her.

"Fuck, that's hot," I murmured and reached down to run the pad of my thumb over her tight little hole. I pushed the digit, now coated with my seed, into her body. "I belong in here," I said, needing her to know that. Giving her ass one more swat, I put my dick back in my pants and helped her up. Her legs were shaky, and I'd be lying if I didn't admit that made me feel proud as hell.

I wanted to tell her she didn't have to go, that she could spend the next week here with me. But I wasn't the type of guy to push something on someone. I knew she had a good time with me, but that didn't mean she'd want to spend the remaining days of her vacation camped out in my bed with my dick between her thighs.

Although that idea was tempting enough for me to say fuck it all and demand she stay. Instead, I picked up the clothes on the floor and handed them back to her.

"How about I feed you, and than we can work on getting you back to your cabin?" Goddammit, I didn't even want to think about her leaving. Vivian looked down at the ground, not saying anything, but finally nodding.

"Yeah, I should probably get back to my place, right?"

Was she asking me, or questioning what she wanted? I didn't know, but I wasn't going to make an ass out of myself and presume anything. I wanted her, but I wanted her to own it as much as I was.

I took a step forward and looked down at her. Her eyes were big, this light blue color, and I wanted nothing more than to kiss her senseless right now. Instead, I just said what I needed to in order for her to understand where I was coming from.

"The last day has been pretty fucking incredible."

I heard her inhale, and then she nodded. "It has." Her voice was soft, maybe like she was hesitant to say anything.

"I don't know you all that well..." I had to smirk, because although I knew her pretty damn intimately, I was sure she knew what I meant. "And you don't really know me, but I'd like to change that." This was a long shot in seeing if she wanted anything more to do with me than what we'd shared, but I was willing to lay it out bare for her.

"You haven't been with a woman in—"

"That has nothing to do with what I want from you, and how I want to get to know you better." And it didn't, I knew that, felt it in my bones. "Before I moved up here I had a girlfriend, thought I was in love even. I did the city thing, the crowded streets and population. I was stuck and didn't see my life going forward the way I wanted it to." Why I was opening myself up to this woman I hardly knew was beyond me, but I wasn't going to let her go without explaining it. She made me feel good, and I wanted to hold onto that. "After the betrayal, I left her and everything else behind. I didn't want any of that shit anymore, even if I'd never seen them again, I just wanted to leave."

"I..." she stopped talking and looked away.

Well, fuck. I scrubbed a hand over my beard and breathed out. I hadn't been with a woman in so long, I must be doing something wrong.

"This is fast," was her response after a few seconds.

"Yeah," was all I said, because it was the truth. She didn't say anything else as she put on her clothes, and the awkwardness seemed to jump in that small time. I'd been inside of her, for fuck sake, so why this silence was awkward was beyond me. "Come on, let me get some food into you." I'd let this go, for now, because I had just dropped a lot in her lap all at once.

But I knew one thing; I couldn't just let her go for good, even if she said this was a one-time deal. If she needed time, fine, I'd give her that. But I wouldn't stay away forever.

I'd had a taste of her, and now I was fucking addicted.

She was mine.

Chapter Nine

Vivian

Ten days later

I stood by my window, stared down at the bustling city beneath me, and felt this oppression fill me. I'd been back home in the city for only a few days, and I felt like I was living in a coffin. After Jake had taken me back to my cabin, it had taken everything in me not to pull Jake into the cabin and spend the rest of my vacation tangled in the sheets with him. But I needed to think, and I had to get my shit in order.

But being back in the city—only three days in—and I was miserable. It just made me feel like I was underwater, and I couldn't hold my breath long enough to reach the surface.

I turned from the window just as a line of cars started honking at each other. Even thought the glass and walls, it sounded loud and suffocating. Since leaving Jake's place, he's all I've thought about, all I wanted to think about.

Grabbing my cell, I pulled up the app for my bank, entered in my information, and stared at my savings balance. Not really having a life aside of work for the last decade, and putting everything extra I made into my savings, I had a nice nest egg. I'd been putting that money away in hopes of one day buying my own place. As the years passed, I just couldn't find the energy to make the commitment to get that house while still having to come into the city.

I tossed my phone on the coffee table, rested my head back on the couch cushion, and closed my eyes. Of course, I imagined Jake in all his manly lumberjack glory. He was just so masculine, and the way he'd worked me over in less than a day had ruined me for any other sexual encounters I might have in the future.

Who am I kidding? I didn't want anyone else but him.

I slowly opened my eyes as reality set in. I didn't have to be trapped, stuck in this coffin-like existence. I could be whoever and whatever I wanted in this life. I only lived once, and why shouldn't I be happy?

All I'd been able to think about since leaving Jake was the words he'd said to me, and how he'd wanted to know me better. It might have been this insta-lust kind of deal between us, but it had been the most real thing I'd ever experienced. It wasn't even just about the sex—although that had been hot as hell. It had been about the way he'd opened me up and made me feel things I'd never experienced before. Jake might never know that, probably hadn't even realized how trapped I'd truly been, but he'd opened my eyes to what I could have.

I grabbed my phone again, dialed my boss's number to tell him I was taking a leave of absence. I could feel the rush move through me. I was feeling all kinds of jittery-goodness. I was doing this, just going to throw caution to the wind, and wherever I landed had to be better than where I was right now.

Jake might know me intimately, but I desperately wanted him to know me as a person, mentally and emotionally. I hoped he was ready for me, because I was about to come at him with everything I had.

Jake

I'd given her enough time to decide what she wanted. I was done standing back and waiting, done having her fill my thoughts all day, only to have the entire process repeat itself when I woke up. She was mine, whether she realized or understood it.

Vivian was mine, and I'd make her see it. She belonged with me out here in the wilderness. If I had to throw her over my shoulder and drag her back here like a caveman, I sure as fuck would.

I parked my truck at the only diner in town, cut the engine, and started running my fingers over the steering wheel. I might be a recluse by choice, but I was familiar with the town and its residents. The way they glanced at me curiously told me being down here was probably a shock, especially since it wasn't time for me to do the monthly grocery run. I stared at the pay phone by the front door and had to shake my head. Before coming to live in the middle of nowhere, I hadn't seen an actual pay phone in longer than I could even remember. But now that I didn't even own a cell phone, this pay phone was my connection to the 'outside' world.

I had a plan in mind, or at least I saw it playing out a certain way. Whether it actually happened that way, I didn't fucking know.

I climbed out of my truck and went to the payphone. I only had her name to go by, but at least I knew she was from the city. But knowing my luck there was probably a dozen women with her name.

And I'll hunt down every single one of them until I find her.

That I'd held back this long when I wanted her so badly was a miracle. It hadn't been about sex for me, not when it was all said and done.

I picked up the pay phone, and just as I was about to dial the operator, I felt someone behind me.

"Jake?"

Her voice shot through me like an electrical current, and instantly, my cock got hard. I hung up the phone and turned around, seeing Vivian standing there, looking up at me like she was just as shocked as I felt.

There was lot I wanted to say, but instead of speaking, I simply went on instinct. I reached out, wrapped my hand around her waist, and pulled her right up against my body. Taking my other hand and gripping her nape, I tilted her head back another inch and stared right into her blue eyes. She melted against me, placed her hands on my chest, and started chuckling. I knitted my brows. My dick was hard, my heart was thundering, and I didn't know what in the hell she could find funny right now.

She smoothed her hands over my shirt. "You wearing flannel makes me think of Mountain Men." Her smile faded as she drew her gaze from my red flannel button down shirt to my eyes. "But then again, that's why I came back; I needed my lumberjack."

Fuck, I couldn't even speak right now; I was so happy she was right here with me.

"I have never felt anything remotely close to what I experienced with you, Jake." She curled her nails against my chest. "And even though I felt that way while I was still tangled in the sheets with you, it wasn't until I got back home that I realized how trapped I'd let myself get." She closed her eyes and rested her forehead in the center of my chest.

I cupped the back of her head and just held her. I saw people looking at us, the shock on their faces clear.

I didn't give a fuck. Hell, I'd bend Vivian over the hood of my truck and fuck her in front of everyone just to show them she was mine.

"I took a leave of absence because I need to see what this is between us and where it might go." She lifted her head and looked at me again. "If that's what you want, too." She didn't give me a chance to say anything before she spoke again. "I'm hoping you holding me like this means you want it, too."

I didn't say anything verbally; I just leaned down and kissed her until she was gasping for air, and her body was pressed hard against mine.

I pulled away and looked at her now pink, swollen lips. "I hope that answers that."

She nodded slowly.

"I'm not letting you go, Vivian." I kissed her again and murmured against her mouth, "You're mine."

Epilogue

Vivian

One year later

When I'd first come back to Jake it had been to see where things might go. Well, twelve months later, I was still here, with no intention of going back to the city. This was where I was happy, and Jake was the man that made my life whole.

I lifted the cup of coffee to my mouth and leaned against the banister on the deck. I watched Jake and a few of the men he worked with cut and measure out the lumber for the addition on the cabin.

My focus was trained on Jake as he leaned down and picked up a raw log and balanced it on one shoulder. Part of the interior of the new addition would have exposed beams and bark detailing. That had been something I'd wanted, and Jake had been more than happy to give it to me. With me having no intention of leaving, and Jake and I talking about marriage and even babies, this one-room cabin wasn't really going to cut it. But neither of us wanted to move, so we were expanding on it and making a few more rooms.

Despite four other men working on the cabin, I was just wearing one of Jake's oversized shirts; I didn't care if they saw me watch my man work. There a nothing more arousing than seeing Jake handle lumber.

He dropped the log by the chopping block, pulled his ax free from the wood, and started working on cutting the timber. He had on a blue flannel shirt this time, the sleeves rolled up his forearms and sweat beading his hairline. It was only eight in the morning, and they'd all been hard at work for the last two hours.

He looked up at me, his ax braced over his shoulder, and gave me a wink. My pussy clenched, got wet, and all I wanted to do was tell him to come inside and fuck me until I passed out. I had never seen myself as a fiend, but Jake brought a whole new meaning to the term.

Maybe he saw the way I looked at him, or maybe the sight of me in his clothes—which I knew turned him on—had his control slipping.

"Take twenty," Jake yelled out to the other guys while still looking at me.

I grinned and moved back from the banister.

In no time at all, he stalked toward me, grabbed me around the waist, and hauled me up against his hard body. He was slightly sweaty, but it was that clean kind of perspiration, the kind I wanted to lick off of him.

"*Only* twenty minutes?" I teased.

He grunted. "Baby, I only need five to get us both off." He kissed me deeply. "The other fifteen is me recovering after fucking you raw." He kissed the side of my neck. "If you haven't realized it yet, you work me over pretty damn hard."

I couldn't even say anything for how aroused I was. But I did pull back and look into his eyes. We had talked about marriage, but I wasn't rushing that. We didn't need a paper to say whom we were meant to be with. I knew Jake was mine, just as much as he knew I was his. We were in this together, and for the long haul.

We also weren't getting any younger, which was something we'd also talked about.

I grinned, and I could see on his expression he knew where I was going with this. "Let's start on that family," I whispered against his ear, and I felt his whole body tense.

He pulled me impossibly tighter against him, and the feeling of his cock, hard, big and thick, pressed against my belly, had a gush of wetness leaving me.

"You sure you want to start that?" he asked me, and all I could do was nod.

"I'm sure." And I was.

"You sure you want my baby growing here," he growled out those words, and placed his hand right on my belly.

A shiver worked through me at the possessiveness in his voice. "I've never been more sure of what I want, Jake, and that's you in my life, and your baby inside of me."

He carried me to the bed and set me in the center. I watched in female appreciation as he took off his flannel shirt, pulled the white t-shirt that had been under it up and over his head, and looked down at me with the intense arousal.

"You're mine, Vivian. You'll always be mine."

Yes I was, and God did it feel good.

The End

VIRGIN

A Real Man, 2

VIRGIN (A Real Man, 2)
By Jenika Snow
www.JenikaSnow.com
Jenika_Snow@Yahoo.com
Copyright © July 2016 by Jenika Snow
First E-book Publication: July 2016

Photographer: Wander Aguiar :: Photography
Cover model: Marshall Perrin
Photo provided by: Wander Book Club

Editor: R. Cartee
Editor: K. Alexander

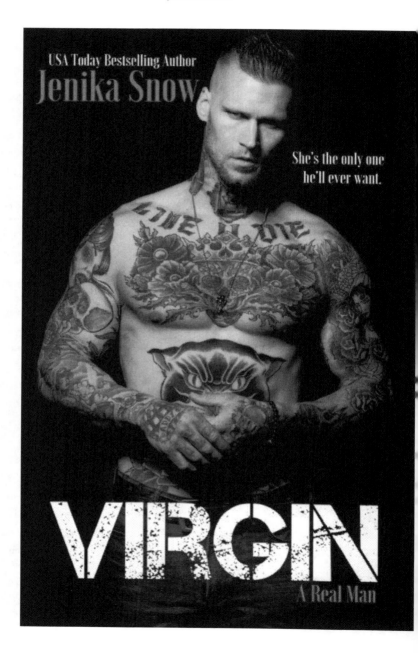

USA Today Bestselling Author
Jenika Snow

She's the only one
he'll ever want.

VIRGIN

A Real Man

She's the only one he'll ever want.
He is the first boy she fell in love with.

Quinn

I met Isabel when I was ten.

I fell in love with her before I even knew what that meant.

I knew from the moment I saw her she was it for me. No one else compared to her, and I'd do anything to make her mine. But I was afraid of losing the friendship we have, so I've kept my mouth shut.

But she's leaving me, and I know I can't keep how I feel inside any longer.

Saving myself for the girl I love isn't a hardship, but it's something I'm proud of. When it comes to Isabel, giving her my virginity, and making her see we belong together, is all that matters.

Isabel

Quinn is like the other half of my soul, the one person I can talk to about anything. He has the bad boy thing going on but is also respectful as much as he is a rebel.

He is the first and only boy I will ever love.

Being forced to move across the country, and leave him behind, is like leaving a piece of myself in the process. But telling Quinn I am madly in love with him could put a strain on our friendship. I don't know if that's something I could handle or risk.

Quinn

Nothing can keep me from Isabel. She is it for me, and I mean that in every conceivable way. Nothing can keep me from her. I hope she's ready because there isn't anything or anyone that will stop me from having her as mine.

Warning: This story is quick and dirty and filled with a virgin hero who wants his heroine to be his one and only. It's drama free, and has insta-everything going on, so be prepared to have an overload of sugary virgin goodness.

Chapter One

Quinn

The first time I saw Isabel, I knew she was something special.

I hadn't even spoken to her, didn't even know her name, but like those sappy songs and movies where they talk about that instant connection ... yeah, I had gone there with her.

We were ten years old, and she was being picked on by some little prick; the sight of her crying had done something to me instantly. I'd wanted to protect her, to hurt anyone that thought they could make her cry.

I'd stormed right over there, pulled her behind me, and given the bullying asshole a black eye.

After that day, we became inseparable.

After that day, no one fucked with her, not unless they wanted to deal with me.

And they never did.

I might not have known what I was feeling for her at such a young age, but I knew without a doubt she was it for me. I wanted her in my life forever.

As the years went on, our relationship became stronger, our friendship tighter. She was my best friend, the one girl I could talk to about anything. And she could do the same with me. But that friendship evolved for me, and I didn't just see myself as her protector anymore, but the guy that didn't want any prick even looking at her.

I knew I loved her before I even knew what that fucking word meant.

We were both eighteen, and although I'd always kept my distance when it came to telling her how I really felt, I knew I couldn't hold that shit in anymore. I loved Isabel so much it hurt.

She'd never know how much she meant to me unless I grew some balls and told her. But I was afraid, afraid of losing the best thing in my life. The fear that I could ruin everything with those three words had kept my mouth shut, but I couldn't do that anymore.

She was the most important person to me. Isabel was my world, my life. Hell, I breathed because of her.

She didn't know it, but she was mine, and I needed to tell her before it was too late.

Isabel

I felt like crying.

They weren't happy tears, but soul numbing, heart-breaking tears that would consume me and not let go until it had wrung every last ounce of energy from me. If I gave in and let that sorrow take over, I'd crumble to the floor and not be able to get back up.

"Everything will work out, Isabel."

I looked at my mom before I walked out of the front door and headed to school. My eyes stung from the unshed tears, and my throat was so dry and tight I couldn't even swallow.

"No, it won't be okay."

My mom gave me a sympathetic look, and I hated it. "Isabel, we didn't mean to spring this on you, but we just found out, as well. Your father can't pass up the promotion, even if it means we have to move your senior year."

I just shook my head. I didn't care if I had to finish my senior year at another school. What I cared about, what was breaking my heart, was the fact I had to tell Quinn about this.

I would be leaving my best friend.

I would be leaving the guy I was hopelessly in love with.

Not saying anything was the best route; if I opened my mouth, I'd either yell at my mom for ruining the best thing in my life, or cry like a little bitch.

I just left the house, got in my car, and drove to school.

Everything passed by in a blur. I was at school before I even realized it. After cutting the engine, I just sat there, my heart racing, my body numb. I didn't know how to tell Quinn any of this.

I don't want to tell him.

Telling myself this was all just an overreaction was easier said than done.

It's just one more year, and we can be together again.

It's just one year of us being apart all the way across the country.

Closing my eyes and resting my head back on the seat, I could have cried at my thoughts.

Be together? Quinn and I were a lot of things, but *together* wasn't one of them. He was my best friend, the boy who had protected me when I was only ten and being picked on. He was the first person to tell me things would be okay because he wouldn't let anyone hurt me. Although my home life was fine, happy even, the very thought of not having Quinn in it, not being able to see him every day, talk to him, and feel so protected because I knew he would never let anything happen to me, was unbearable.

When I opened my eyes, I saw Quinn walking toward the car. He always waited for me so we could walk together, and knowing I'd have to finish off my last year of school without doing this one thing every day broke my heart.

But I plastered on a smile, because I didn't want to tell him right now and ruin the entire day. It was Friday and I could tell him after school; that way we'd have the whole weekend to hang out, maybe talk about this.

"Hey," he said and leaned his massive biceps on the inside of the window, his smile bright, straight, and white.

"Hey yourself." I smiled wider, turned to grab my bag off the passenger seat, and went to open my door, but he was already there doing it for me. Once out of the car, I tried to keep my composure happy, but inside I was a wreck.

I stared up at him, his body massive for only being eighteen. He had tattoos on his arms, even though he was younger. He appeared like the bad boy in all ways, was in many senses, but he was also my best friend.

He played hockey, and his body was a machine, tearing through anything and anyone to get what he wanted. At six foot three and two hundred pounds of raw muscle, Quinn didn't look like someone that should be going to this rinky-dink little high school. He looked like a man in many ways.

He was a hard ass to all others, but to me he was the sweetest person. He showed me a side that he didn't allow anyone else to see, and that made me love him even harder.

One of his friends who also played hockey came over and started "talking shop" with him, and I just stared up at him. His dark blond hair was cut short and had a mussed look going on. From this angle, his light blue eyes almost looked crystalline. And the clothes he wore ... yeah, they couldn't hide the raw power he exuded. Big biceps, vein-roped forearms. He was perfection, and I wanted him to be mine.

God, what am I doing, measuring him for a suit?

How am I going to get through this, even if it is for only one year?

Chapter Two

Quinn

I could tell something was wrong with her as soon as I saw her this morning. She was being fake and had plastered on a tight smile, but in her eyes, I could see something was bothering her.

My first instinct was to demand she tell me who the fuck hurt her, because I was ready to beat that fucker down, but I kept my cool, wanting her to come to me and tell me what was wrong.

I sat in my seat in the back of the class, staring at her, unable to focus on what the teacher said. Isabel sat a few seats in front of me and to the right. She kept tapping her pencil on the desk and bouncing her leg, her nerves clear. I'd never really seen her like this, and it had every muscle in my body taut with the need to make things right for her, to make her feel better.

She looked back at me then, maybe feeling my stare burning a hole in the back of her head. She smiled, but it was tight and didn't reach her eyes. I curled my hands into tight fists, wanting to just fuck the class and drag her out of the room, but thankfully the bell for the end of the day rang. I shot out of my seat, grabbed my backpack, and stormed over to her.

"Hey," she said softly as she put her books in her bag. I saw the column of her throat work as she swallowed, could see how tight her jaw was.

"Come on," I said and all but dragged her out of the classroom, down the hall, and finally outside.

We made our way to her car, and only then did I cross my arms and glare down. I waited for her to tell me what the fuck was going on, and when she didn't, I exhaled.

"What's gong on?" I asked, making my voice softer. I didn't want to upset her because frankly, I was on edge not knowing what was going on with her. She never kept things from me.

"What do you mean?" she asked, but she didn't meet my eyes.

I placed my forefinger under her chin and tilted her head back. "Isabel," I said in a low voice. "What's going on?" She didn't answer me right away, and when I saw the tears start forming in her eyes, I cursed. "Did someone fuck with you?" I curled the hand not touching her into a fist and gritted my teeth. I needed to stay calm, because the very thought of someone messing with her had me nearly going off the rails.

"If someone fucked with you, so help me God..." I shook my head. "I'll make them hurt." I stared into her hazel eyes, could see her mahogany colored hair blowing around her shoulders. Hell, I could smell the citrusy scent that always surrounded her. Despite not knowing what was up with her, I was getting hard, wanting her like a fiend wanting a hit of my addiction.

She shook her head. "No one hurt me, Quinn." Her voice was low, distant almost.

I wanted to smooth my thumb along the soft skin under her chin, but I refrained and pulled my hand away. "You've been acting weird all day. Tell me what's wrong, because I know you well enough that I can see you're bothered."

She looked at the ground and closed her eyes. After a second, she lifted her head and looked me right in the eyes. God, she was gorgeous; even looking like someone had ripped her heart out and stomped on it, she was the most beautiful fucking person I'd ever seen. I wanted to pull her in and kiss her until she was breathless, wanted to tell her I loved her, and that I was so fucking in love with her I lay in bed at night thinking about her being mine.

I wanted to tell Isabel she was it for me ... that she was the only one I'd ever want.

I was a virgin, and I wanted Isabel to be my first and last.

"We're moving, Quinn."

Her words brought me back to the present, had me blinking and trying to process what she'd said. "What?" I asked, hearing her, knowing what she said, but not comprehending it.

"I'm moving. My dad got a promotion, and relocating is part of it." She brushed away a tear that fell from her eye.

"Moving?" I asked, my voice thick, tight.

She nodded.

I shook my head. "When?"

She was silent for long moments, and I felt myself become tighter, knowing what she was going to say would be fucking hell.

"Less than two weeks."

I felt the breath leave me. I couldn't do anything but stand there and stare at her, watching as the tears slid down her cheeks.

"Two fucking weeks?" I gritted those words out. "Are you serious?"

She nodded.

Reaching up, because I couldn't stand to see her crying, to see her hurt, I cupped her cheek and brushed two tears away with my thumb.

"How the hell can anyone move in two weeks?" I meant to say those words to myself, but they spilled forth. "Fuck," I said and squeezed my eyes shut.

We hadn't been apart for more than a day since we were ten.

I fucking loved her.

I love you.

She cupped my hand, neither of us speaking or moving for long moments. Finally, she sighed and smiled, but it was sad.

"The position my dad is taking needs to be filled right away." Her voice was soft. "And my mom doesn't want to wait a year until I'm done with school to move out there. She wants to be with my dad."

Yeah, I got that, understood it even, but hell, what about us?

It was then, as those words sunk in, that I felt rage fill me. I felt this bone-deep anger that took my breath away, that stole every single ounce of sanity. I wanted to avenge her even if there wasn't a monster in front of her, wasn't someone that had stolen an ounce of her flesh. I wanted to be the one to hold her close and keep her by me, making sure she couldn't be hurt, not by her family ... not by a distance that was the enemy.

I wanted to tell her right then that everything would be okay, that I'd never walk away from her. I'd follow her to the end of the fucking world if I had to.

She was it for me, and tonight I'd tell her how I felt.

Tonight, I'd take her somewhere private, where it was just us, and tell her my deepest secret.

Tonight I'd tell Isabel that I loved her, and nothing would keep us apart.

Chapter Three

Isabel

"Have you told Quinn?" my father asked from across the dinner table.

"Yeah," I replied in a dead tone.

"Honey, eat," my mother said.

I stared at my plate, pushing my food around with my fork. They actually expected me to eat, to have an appetite after the shit they threw at me this morning?

"I'm not hungry." I set my fork down and looked at the clock. I was meeting Quinn in twenty minutes. He wanted us to hang out, to spend time together, and really talk about all of this. At least the latter was what I assumed.

"It's for one year, Isabel," my dad said, sounding frustrated. I didn't care if he was annoyed. "Once you graduate, if you want to go to school here, or wherever Quinn is, that's an option."

"A year is a long time," I said, my voice monotone, and I knew my expression reflected that. "Let's not forget you're uprooting me during my senior year, or that we have to move across the country." I straightened, not about to cry at the dinner table. "It's not like I'm moving to the next city over. It's not like I can tell Quinn to go with me."

My dad exhaled and grabbed his napkin to wipe his mouth. When he set it down, he looked me right in the eyes. "I know you and Quinn are close. And I know this will be a hard adjustment. But it's for one year, honey, and I can't pass up this promotion." He said the last part a little softer. "I've been working toward this for the last ten years."

I wanted to support my dad, knew he deserved this, but it was hard to feel any kind of happiness toward anyone when I was hurting so much.

"I'm sorry. I'm happy you're getting what you deserve, but it's ... hard for me." I stood and walked over to the table in the foyer. I gabbed my keys from the little bowl on it and stared at myself in the mirror above the table. I looked like shit, with dark circles under my eyes and this shitty expression covering my face. I might only be five minutes away from where I was to meet Quinn, and I'd obviously be early, but I'd rather sit there with just my thoughts and the silence than stay here and try and be happy when I wasn't.

"Where are you going?" my mother asked.

"To spend time with my best friend."

And the boy I love.

Quinn

I'd been sitting on the roof of my car for the last hour, even if Isabel wasn't supposed to show up for a while still. I just needed to get my thoughts in order. I'd pushed everything aside that had to do with her leaving, because tonight, I wanted her to know how special she was to me, how much she meant to me.

I wanted to tell her I loved her, and that no matter where she went, or how far away it was, I would find her. Our lives would always be entwined, no matter what.

The flash of headlights had me turning and looking over my shoulder. This strip of property was out in the middle of nowhere, with cornfields stretching out in front of me for miles, and the open sky making way to the thousand of stars above.

I'd never been one of those sappy guys that cared about feelings or any of that shit. I didn't care about any of that stuff with anyone aside for Isabel.

We'd been coming here since we were old enough to drive. It was the one spot we could talk unfiltered, without the outside world intruding.

She pulled her car behind mine and cut the engine. I'd wanted to pick her up at her folks' house, wanted to do this right, but she'd insisted on meeting me here. My first thought was she wanted an escape route if things got too emotional or real, even if she didn't exactly know what I planned on telling her tonight.

When she got out of the car, I slid off the hood of mine and walked over to her. Her face lit up when she saw me, and that made me feel so fucking good. All she had to do was smile at me, and I fucking crumbled.

Tonight, she'd find out that for her, I'd do anything.

Tonight, she'd find out that I'd fall to my knees and worship her if that's what would make her happy.

I embraced her before she could even say anything, and at first she was tense, but then she melted into me. We stood there like that for so long, but I didn't want to pull away. I didn't want this moment to end.

"This fucking sucks," she said against my shirt. I was so much taller than she was, her head resting right under my pectoral. I liked that she was so tiny compared to me, and that I could hold her close and nearly engulf her. It made me feel like nothing in this world could touch her, that as long as she was with me, everything would be okay.

"They keep telling me it's only for a year until I finish school." She pulled away and looked up at me. She wasn't crying, but she was on the verge. I cupped her cheeks and kissed her forehead.

I was only like this with her.

I didn't care what others said about me, or if my friends gave me a hard time and said I was too soft when it came to Isabel. I didn't give a shit about any of that, or about what they had to say, because when all was said and done, the only person that mattered to me was looking right into my eyes.

"I'll go with you," I said with determination, not sure how I'd get that to work out seeing as the part-time job I had wasn't exactly padding my savings account.

She smiled and shook her head. "That's dumb," she said and laughed, and I knew she wasn't insulting me.

"I would, though, Isabel," I said in all seriousness. The smile faded from her face. "I'd follow you to the end of the world just to make sure we stayed together." My heart was thundering, and despite the fact we weren't *together*, I wanted her to know she meant everything to me.

"As much as I love the idea of you going with me and toughing this next year out, I wouldn't want you to do that, Quinn." She pulled away and stared up at the sky. "Have you ever thought about how tiny we really are?" A moment of silence passed before she spoke again. "Have you ever really thought that out of the entire world, the universe, the great blankness above us, that we are just these little specks of cells and energy?"

I heard what she said, but I was too focused on her, at the way she looked staring up at the sky, at the vulnerability and sadness I saw on her face.

"It's only a year of school before we can be together again, but it feels like someone is ripping out my heart, Quinn." She looked at me then, that vulnerability so raw, so real, that I felt it in every cell in my body. "I know to outsiders looking in I'm being dramatic, but I can't help it. I love—"

"I love you, Isabel," I said, cutting her off, not about to hold this in anymore. She didn't move, didn't even show emotion for long moments. "I am so fucking in love with you, and have been before I even know what that emotion was." I cupped her face again and leaned down so we were eye to eye. "Ever since I met you when we were ten, I felt something in me start to grow. As the years went on, that affection grew to what I feel now."

I heard her gasp a little, just a tiny sound that left her lips parted, but I wasn't going to stop. I couldn't. Now that the words were out, hanging between us, I wanted to lay it all bare.

"I didn't want to say anything before because I was afraid of ruining the friendship we have. Having you in my life, even if only as a friend, is what I'll take, because the alternative isn't an option for me, Isabel."

Chapter Four

Isabel

I couldn't breathe, but right now that wasn't a bad thing. The fact Quinn had just opened himself up to me, and told me exactly what I'd always longed to hear, had the world rushing around me. I felt lightheaded, my hands shook, and it felt as though my knees would lock if I tried to step away.

"You love me?" I asked stupidly. The fact was I was shocked he'd admitted this stuff to me. For so long, I'd loved him, but *I* hadn't wanted to ruin our friendship by telling him how I felt. And if he hadn't felt the same way, there would have been this awkward wall between us.

He held on to each side of my face, his blue eyes looking intense ... sincere. "I fucking love you so much it pains me, Isabel. I've wanted to tell you for so long."

I wanted to cry tears of happiness, but I also knew this made things a little worse. He loved me. I loved him. The separation would be so much worse now.

But will it?

"Did I just fuck things up?" he whispered, his voice deep, filled with emotion.

Shit, I hadn't said anything in return. "You didn't fuck anything up," I whispered. "I'm so in love with you, Quinn. I've kept it to myself, too, afraid it might ruin the closeness we had if you didn't feel the same way."

He grinned, his straight white teeth flashing. Quinn crushed me to his body, and I closed my eyes, inhaling his woodsy, masculine scent, just letting him hold me and make things seem not so shitty. I'd agreed to come out here tonight not just to talk to him, but also to finally admit things, even if it would ruin things. Me having to move put a lot of shit into perspective.

What would it have hurt anyway? If that wedge had been put between us, it wouldn't have mattered because we already had distance.

"You're the only one I've ever wanted," he said and pulled away to look into my face. "You're the only one I'll ever want."

My heart was in my throat. Quinn was a tough guy. I'd seen him on the ice, watched as he dominated it, took down the other team. Hell, if they hadn't been forced to play against him, I knew they probably would have parted for him, just let him have his way. School was no different either.

But right here, right now, he was so open to me. He'd also been sweet and gentle with me, as if I might break, but right now, yeah, this was a side I'd never seen.

"I've never wanted anyone else, Isabel," he said softly. "It's only ever been you. I've wanted you in my life not just as my best friend, but as the girl I want to give every part of myself to. It's you I want to own my virginity. It's you I want to share my life with."

I couldn't think, couldn't even breathe after he spoke. I'd saved myself for him too, and although I'd never seen him with any girls, the truth was I'd never wanted to think too hard on it either. I'd never wanted to picture the guy I loved being physical with anyone but me.

But to know he was a virgin, that he'd saved himself for me, the same as I'd done for him, made my emotions rise up violently. I didn't want to think anymore, didn't want to worry about leaving or how hard it was going to be.

All I wanted to do was be with Quinn in the most basic of ways and show him how much I loved him by sharing my body.

Quinn

She was close to me already, but when she rose on her toes, pressed her chest to mine, and I felt the curved roundness of her breasts, my cock jerked something fierce. But it didn't stop there, and as surprised as I was by her actions, I held her tightly.

She stared right in my eyes, both of us breathing the same air. My heart was beating like a freight train, and I felt my pulse slam hard against my skin. I wanted to kiss her, to have her in the ways I'd always dreamed of.

I might be a virgin, but I knew what I wanted to do with Isabel, and fuck, was it filthy.

But just as I was about to act on what I wanted, Isabel slammed her mouth against mine. At first, neither of us moved, but then I took control. I cupped the back of her head, tangled my fingers in her hair, and tilted her head so I could thrust my tongue in her mouth. I groaned this guttural sound, the flavor of her like nothing I'd ever tasted before.

I wrapped my other arm snuggly around her waist and used my strength to lift her off the ground a couple of inches, just holding her, loving that she was pressed all up against me. I knew she could feel my cock, and I wondered what she was thinking.

I stroked my tongue along hers, and when she pulled it farther into her mouth and bit down on it gently, I couldn't help but thrust my cock deeper into her belly, digging the fucker into her softness.

"Be with me, Quinn."

Holy. Fuck.

I froze after she murmured those words and broke the kiss to look down at her face. I set her on the ground, but kept my arm wrapped around her, wanting her close.

Her mouth was swollen and red, and a light sheen of salvia covered her lips. I felt so fucking possessive of her, and I couldn't help but untangle my hands from her hair and run my finger over her bottom lip.

She parted her lips slightly, darted out her tongue, and ran it over the pad of the digit. "Be with me, Quinn," she whispered again, and I felt my cock jerk. If the motherfucker could have spoken, he would have been growling his approval. I was all for being with Isabel, too, but I didn't want to rush anything.

"Baby, I don't want you to feel like we have to do this because you're leaving. I'm not going anywhere." I cupped her nape. "I told you, you're mine and nothing will change that."

She shook her head. "I've wanted to be with you like this for a long time. We're alone, I love you, and it feels like the right time."

God, I could have come right in my fucking jeans listening to her say these things to me. I wanted her, but I also wanted to make sure she wasn't rushing anything because our emotions were raw and wild.

"Please, let's make this a memory I can take with me when I have to go."

Fuck, my heart broke, but I wasn't about to say no either. I crushed her to me again, speared my hands in her hair, and kissed her until she was gasping for breath and clinging to me.

Turning us around, I walked us backward until the car stopped us from going farther. She had her back to the driver's side window, and I curled my bigger body around hers, causing her to arch for me. Her breasts were more than a handful, but fit her slender body perfectly. My fingers itched to touch them, to unbutton her shirt, pull the sides apart, and just go to town massaging the globes.

"Touch me," she whispered, as if she read my mind.

I was about to fucking come right in my jeans, no joke, but I needed to keep my cool. I might be a virgin, but I'd jerked off plenty of times to the image of Isabel in my head, enough that I had self-control down pretty damn well.

I pulled back, forcing myself to break the kiss. Before I undid her shirt, I ran my tongue over first her top lip and then her bottom. She moaned, and I couldn't help kissing her again, swallowing the sound. Finally, I took a step back, clenching my hands into fists repeatedly as I watched the rise and fall of her breasts under the light pink blouse she wore.

"Please." She whispered that word on a moan, and my fucking control snapped right in half.

I all but tore those little pearl buttons off, parted the material, and stared down at the white bra she wore. My mouth dry, the fucker in my pants throbbed. Hell, the bra wasn't anything fancy, just cotton with a little lace detailing around the edges. But the fucking material was transparent, and I could make out the quarter-sized areolae. They were a darker red, and her nipples were hard and pressed against the fabric.

"*Christ*, Isabel." I dragged my gaze up and looked at her face. Pleasure was clear on her expression. I didn't want to be crude or too rough, but I didn't know if I could control myself to be tame.

The truth was that jerking off and actually standing in front of Isabel, about to be with her, was really fucking different.

No shit.

"You look scared," she said softly, and I breathed out slowly.

"I'm not scared, baby. I'm trying not to devour you." When I opened my eyes, she made this little sound in the back of her throat. I wondered what I looked like to her.

"Maybe I want that." Her words were heady, softly spoken, and told me exactly how much she wanted this.

"Once I start, I won't be able to stop." I wanted to be honest.

"I won't ask you to stop."

Good. God.

"Giving up your virginity doesn't have to be with candles and sweet words."

My throat tightened as she spoke.

"It can be raw and animalistic."

Was this my Isabel, the sweet and softly spoken girl I was in love with?

"Is that how you want it from me, for our first time?" To be honest, it didn't matter how I took Isabel for the first time. It wasn't the how it happened, just the fact I was finally having her after all this time.

"I just want you."

If that's how she wanted it, hell, I'd give her so much she couldn't handle it.

Chapter Five

Isabel

My body was on fire, my skin prickled, and all I wanted was Quinn. The way he looked at me was crazy, possessive, and like he was about to tear right through his skin.

That's about how I felt right now, like I couldn't breathe unless I reminded myself to.

But I also thought he might be nervous, maybe thinking I only wanted this because of what was going on. Yes, this was pretty sudden after just saying what we'd said to each other, but this moment seemed perfect, and I didn't want anything to fuck it up, not even worry that I didn't want this.

"I want this. I want you," I said again with more strength. I needed him to know that without a doubt, this was what I wanted.

He made this low sound deep within his chest, something akin to a growl, and then he was on me, his hands on my chest, his mouth at my neck. He shifted slightly and I felt his erection digging into my belly: a huge, thick rod that had my pussy clenching. I was wet, obscenely so, and I knew that before I finally felt him deep in me, I'd only be more soaked.

"Show me where you want me to touch you, Isabel," Quinn said, his voice a husky growl against the side of my throat.

My hands were shaking, but I lifted one of them, grabbed Quinn's much larger hand, and slowly pushed it down between our bodies. He was breathing so hard, his warm breath moving along my skin, making me even more flushed. I don't know what had gotten into me, but I didn't want slow, didn't want romantic or gentle, even though maybe I should have for our first time. I wanted to be with Quinn, the guy I loved, and I didn't care how it transpired as long as it happened right now.

I placed his hand on my lower belly and froze. I heard my heart thundering in my ears, felt it in my throat.

"Do it, baby," he whispered by my ear. "Show me where you want me."

I pushed his hand lower, until it was right between my thighs. Could he feel how wet I was? Did he know that slight pressure of his palm on my pussy felt incredible?

He groaned and thrust his cock against my belly.

"You want me right here, baby?"

I nodded. This was so surreal, finally being with Quinn, but God, did it feel so right. He stated to rub his palm up and down, and despite the fact I wore jeans, I felt the electricity slam into me. My clit throbbed, like my heart was right there, beating rapidly. I didn't want foreplay, didn't want to take our time. I felt feverish and needy, and I wanted Quinn now.

I pushed him away, and he groaned. Lowering my gaze to the crotch of his pants, I saw the huge outline of his erection pressing against his jeans. God, he looked huge. I went for the button and zipper of my jeans, and once those were undone, I pushed the denim down my thighs.

He shook his head. "I should have you on a warm bed, Isabel, not out there in a field up against my car."

"What does it matter as long as we are together?"

He groaned again. "You're killing me here." He reached down and palmed himself through his jeans.

"Let me see it," I whispered, feeling so bold; I wasn't acting like my shy self.

He didn't move for a long while, but finally I heard his zipper going down and lowered my gaze to what he was about to show me.

When he pulled his cock out, I felt my heart jump into my throat. He was huge, thick and long, and the crown slightly wider than the rest of him. He had his palm wrapped around his dick and he stroked himself, his focus on my chest.

I wanted to touch it, to see if it was just as hard and smooth as it looked. Without thinking about it anymore, I walked the few steps to get to him, pushed his hand aside, and stared into his eyes.

"Touch me, Isabel," Quinn said, his voice husky.

I did just that. I wrapped my hand around his length and watched his eyes become hooded, his mouth slack. I started rubbing my palm up and down the big length. His cock was just as hard as it looked, and the skin was warm and smooth; I moved over the length easily.

"I'm about to fucking lose it, Isabel."

I sucked in a deep breath. "I've already lost it for you, Quinn."

And then he had me pulled close to him, had his mouth on mine, and fucked me with his lips and tongue. There was no other word to describe what he was doing to me at this moment. We backed up to the car, and I found myself leaning back against the hood. We made out for long seconds, but when he pulled away and stepped back, I couldn't move, couldn't even ask why he stopped. I heard gravel crunching under his feet and he walked away, and then I heard the trunk open and close. When he was beside me again, he helped me off the hood, spread the blanket he'd grabbed on the ground, and then he helped me down.

My back was against the soft blanket, and the hardness of Quinn's body was over mine. This part of the ground he'd chosen was flat enough that it wasn't uncomfortable, but I was so damn aroused I don't think I would have fully felt any discomfort anyway.

The truth was I'd never imagined a specific experience that would be my first time. The only thing I ever saw was that it would be with Quinn.

This was going to happen right now, and I couldn't think of a more perfect time or place.

I was meant to be with him.

Chapter Six

Quinn

"Are you sure about this, Isabel?" I adjusted my much larger frame over the girl I loved more than anything else and braced my weight on my elbows beside her head. This wasn't exactly where I thought she deserved to have her virginity taken, but just being with her was good enough for me. If this was what she wanted, it was hers.

"I'm more than sure," she said, and arched her chest. Fuck, I was barely holding on to my sanity right now. My cock was so damn hard, and pre-cum was a steady constant at the tip of my cock.

Without talking about it anymore, I rose up to help her out of her shirt and bra, did the same with her panties and the pants that were pooled around her legs, and finished with getting myself naked. I had to admit being out in the middle of nowhere, with the star splattered sky above us, was romantic.

Her cheeks were tinged pink from her arousal, and her lips were swollen and glossy from our making out. I wanted to suck on the flesh, gently nibble on it, and make her come from that alone.

I couldn't help myself. I leaned down and kissed her. She was sweet and addictive, and I knew I'd never get enough. I placed my hand over her bared pussy and she arched, gasping out. "This is mine, Isabel." The possessive side of me rose up like this fierce beast. I wanted her to know, to really fucking see what she did to me.

Her pussy was hot and wet, and when I ran my fingers through her slit, I had to pray I wouldn't come before I was even inside of her.

I lifted enough so that I could look down at her face, and the way she looked up at me, so dreamy and needy, had me growing like some kind of fucking animal. My chest tightened and my cock jerked.

I heard her swallow and saw her throat work. And then she had her hand between our bodies, moving lower, over my abdomen, and causing my muscles to clench.

God, was she going to touch me again?

And then she was gripping me in her palm, and I hung my head and closed my eyes.

"So. Fucking. Good."

She moved her hand up and down my length, paying attention to the crown. I knew she felt all the pre-cum, but her little sounds told me she liked it, liked I was so fucking worked up for her.

"You're so hard." Her voice was so very low and heated from her arousal.

Shit, she couldn't say that kind of stuff to me, not unless she wanted me to blow my load before we even got started.

"I'm hard for you." I opened my eyes. "Only you."

After this night, I knew a lot of shit would come between us, but I was serious when I told her nothing would separate us.

Even if we had to be apart for a year, I would come for her. I would come after her, because she was mine.

I leaned down again, took her mouth in another hard, deep kiss, and just focused on making her feel good. Isabel moved her hand from between our bodies, gripped my biceps with her small hands, and dug her nails into my flesh. Fuck, but she felt so damn good.

Isabel opened her mouth wider, and I plunged my tongue inside, fucking her with slow sweeps of the muscle. With gentle licks on the inside of her mouth, I wanted to make her so ready for me there would me no resistance when I finally had my virgin cock in her virgin pussy.

The wet sound of our kiss filled my head, causing me to feel drunk, high … shit, all of the above. She panted against my mouth, spread her legs wider, and I pressed my hips farther into hers. Gently, slowly, thrusting against her, my cock sliding through her soaked, slick cunt. God, I was losing my mind. My balls were drawn up to my body, and the need to just let go and come was pretty fucking strong. It was through sheer will alone—and the fact I wanted inside her so badly—that I was keeping it together.

I wanted us sweating, panting out in exertion as I claimed her, as she took my virginity, and I owned hers.

As I stared down at her breasts, my mouth watered at the sight of those red, hard nipples almost begging for me to suck on them. It overrode everything else in me. It was hard to go slow, take my time, and fully enjoy this while not rushing and giving her pleasure too. My body screamed to reach down and grab my cock, place it at her entrance, and pop her cherry at the same time I gave her mine.

I dipped my head low and dragged my tongue over one stiff peak, did the same thing to the other, and felt her jerk beneath me. That act had her pussy sliding up and down for a second on my cock, and I groaned. I pulled one hard tip into my mouth and sucked, her flavor sweet, addicting, and like nothing I'd ever had before. I could suck on her forever, just bathe myself in her scent and taste, but she was murmuring for more, to have me take her.

How could I deny my girl when I was being selfish in taking what I needed? I pulled back and watched as she licked her lips. I was riveted to the sight of her bottom lip as it became wet and red from the act.

"Spread your legs wider for me, baby."

I leaned back and braced my hands on the blanket beside her. A bed would obviously be more comfortable, but if my girl was into it then this is how it would be.

I lowered my head and ran my gaze along her belly, over the top of her mound covered by trimmed darker hair, and stared at what she'd revealed.

"God," I said and ran a hand over my mouth. "You're fucking gorgeous here." I ran my finger down her slit, her body trembling for me.

Her pussy lips were wet, pink, and swollen for me. It was all for me.

"You're mine, Isabel." My voice was harsh and gruff.

"I am yours," she whispered.

"You were mine before you knew it." I felt like some kind of animal right now, ready to mark my mate, to make it known that she was mine no matter what. I wanted to lick every inch of her body, wanted to memorize every dip and curve of her, but right now I needed to be inside of her.

I grabbed my cock, stroked myself a few times, and finally placed the tip at her entrance. She smelled so fucking good, like sweet musk that drove me insane.

That scent, the way she was so primed, was all for me.

"You're fucking mine," I said again, staring into her eyes. In one swift move, I buried my nearly ten inches into her wet, tight pussy.

"Oh, God," she whispered and gripped the blanket beside her. Her eyes were wide, her mouth open. I stilled, my balls pressed against her ass, her inner muscle clenching around me. I wanted to fill her with my cum, watch it slip out of her when I pulled out. I wanted her to smell like me, and let every male know that they couldn't have her. I stared down at where we were connected and rubbed my finger along her engorged clit, and lower still until I circled her pussy hole that I filled. Before I could pull away, she grabbed my wrist and pulled that soaked finger to her mouth. I watched with a slack jaw as she sucked on my finger, running her tongue along the digit and cleaning her juices off.

I was going to fill her up with so much of my jizz, my scent, there would be no washing me off of her.

Chapter Seven

Isabel

The pain was instant as soon as Quinn shoved all those inches into me. But I didn't want to show that discomfort on my face; I knew he'd worry, wanting to make sure I was okay.

But the pain was inevitable.

Pain made a lasting impression and was like a wonderful scar laced along the body, a reminder of what was shared, of what was experienced.

Without that pain, it might have well just been another experience for me.

I held onto his biceps, his muscles pronounced, bulging. I dug my nails in, bit my lip, and waited for him to start moving.

And then he did, his huge body shaking above me, the sinews and tendons stretched and taut under his tattooed, golden flesh.

A shock of pain went through me when he started to push back into my body.

"Is it good for you, Isabel?" he asked in a strained voice. "Because it's really fucking good for me." He was thrusting in and out of me, slow, easy, and I knew he didn't want to cause me any unjust pain. But I didn't care if it hurt, because I knew it would morph into pleasure.

"It's good, Quinn." And it wasn't a lie.

He kissed the top of my head and continued to push into me.

In.

Out.

Slow.

Easy.

The feeling of being completely filled by Quinn wasn't something I would have ever been able to envision. I might have thought about it, fantasied about what it would be like, but the real thing was so much more incredible.

And when he pressed his upper body against mine, my softness to his hardness, I sighed. He cupped both sides of my face and kissed me possessively. My pussy clenched around him, and he grunted.

"Fuck..." Quinn moaned that lone word out, and really started moving then, a little faster, a little harder. "You feel..." he gasped out when I clenched around him again. "I never thought it would feel like this." He pulled out and the broad head was poised at my entrance. After a second, he pushed in nice and slow, filling me so completely I felt tears of pleasure in the corner of my eyes.

"Say you're mine," he said softly, his focus on my eyes.

With every inch he sank into me, I felt filled, claimed. I felt owned in every conceivable way.

I didn't hesitate. "I'm yours, Quinn."

He leaned back slightly and watched himself push into me and pull back out.

"Watch me, Isabel." He titled his head slightly so he was able to look at me. "Watch as you take my virginity and I take yours."

I rose up on my elbows, my chest rising and falling as the arousal and experience overwhelmed me. I looked down the length of my body and watched in erotic wonder at what was going on.

The massive, thick length of him slid in and out of my body, and although there wasn't any lighting aside from the moon, it was full and bright, and I could see everything.

"Fuck, look at that, baby." He pulled out several inches, and I saw the streaks of blood on his shaft. Quinn reached out and rubbed his finger along the length, smearing the blood and wetness. When he lifted his hand, my heart stopped.

God, would he do it?

With his eyes locked on mine, I watched as he lifted that finger to his lips and sucked it into his mouth. I felt my mouth part at that incredibly intimate act.

"I know I said it already, but you taste so fucking sweet." He started pushing in and put of me again. "This means mine." He thrust deep into me, and I gasped. "This is irreversible, Isabel. You are tied to me. You are mine no matter what." He thrust deep inside once more, and I closed my eyes, moaning. "This sweet fucking virgin pussy will only ever be mine."

"God, yes."

"I'm yours as much as you're mine." He growled out the words and thrust back into me. "Open your eyes. Watch me fuck you."

I opened my eyes.

The play of muscles that rippled along his shoulders and biceps spoke of his strength, and a gush of moisture slipped from me, further aiding in his penetration. He pulled out slowly and pushed back in. Over and over, he did this, slow and easy thrusts that had me lifting my hips in hopes he'd go deeper, faster.

We were sweaty, both of us panting.

I wanted his sweat to drip on me as he owned me, and that's exactly what he was doing ... owning me.

"I love you," he whispered.

I lifted my gaze to his face to see he was already staring at me. I cupped his cheek. "I love you, too."

His movements picked up. His cock slid in and out of me, growing faster and faster as his hips slapped against mine. The sound of our sexes slapping together filled my head.

"*Christ*," Quinn said harshly and tilted his head back, his neck muscles straining. His was making these deep sounds, and when he looked at me again, it was only for a second. He lowered his gaze down the length of my body so he could see where she was impaled.

Good. Fucking. God.

That was hot as fuck.

And when he placed his thumb on my clit, and started rubbing it back and forth, I exploded for him.

"Fuck. Yeah." Quinn didn't relent as he thrust in and out of me, drawing my orgasm to the peak and keeping it there until I couldn't breathe. I'd gotten off before when I'd touched myself, but this was unlike anything I'd ever felt.

When I came back to reality and opened my eyes, it was to see the untamed look on Quinn's face. Sweat slid down his chest, and I watched the droplets, wanting to rise up and lick them off.

Do it.

I braced my upper body on my elbows and ran my tongue over the beads, tasting the saltiness that was all Quinn. He groaned and bucked against me harder. Grunts and groans left him and grew louder the more he pumped into me.

"I'm so close, but I want this to last."

I rested on my back again and slid my hands up his biceps and framed his neck. "Just let go."

He groaned harshly again.

"Oh, God, Isabel." He looked so tight, his body strained, his expression almost pained. "I love you so fucking much. I can't let you go," he panted out. "I can't let you walk away from me." He thrust in deep and grunted low. "You and I were meant to be together."

I was going to come again. And when I saw his pleasure start to morph, his control slipping, I let myself go once more. The explosion inside of me rivaled the one before. My pussy clamped down hard around him just as he buried himself to the hilt in me, moaning as he came. He shook above me, his eyes squeezed shut as he filled me up.

When he relaxed on top of me, our sweaty skin rubbed along each other. Before I could tell him he was suffocating me with his weight, he rolled off and pulled me in close. I didn't even care the hardness of the car pushed into my very bones. Closing my eyes and resting my forehead on his damp chest, I listened to the sound of his heart beating.

I felt Quinn stroking his fingers up and down my back, and as nice as it felt, I wanted to make sure he was okay with what we'd done. I pushed up and braced myself on an elbow, staring down at him. For a second, he just stared at me, and then lifted his hand to cup my cheek, the corner of his mouth curled up slightly in a smile.

"Hey," he said, his voice thicker.

"Hi," I whispered and leaned down to kiss him. As the pleasure and experience faded, the reality of everything crashed back in. I knew Quinn sensed it too because he stilled.

"Everything will work out."

I looked him in the eyes.

"I'll make sure it works out in the end, because a life without you isn't conceivable." He leaned up and kissed me on the forehead. "If I can't fight for my love for you, what's the point?" When he pulled back, I saw that vulnerability once more. "I've never loved anyone the way I love you, and I'm not about to let that go. It might not be until we finish out this year, and maybe you'll be thousands of miles away, but you're mine, and nothing can change that. I meant it when I said I wouldn't let anyone or anything take you away from me."

Hearing Quinn say that made me feel like everything would be okay.

It had to be, right?

He shifted slightly, his focus trained on me. "There isn't anything I wouldn't do for you, Isabel." His tone was so sure, so controlled. He cupped my face and leaned down so we were eye-to-eye. "You're it for me. You've always been it for me."

God, things had to work out. They just had to.

Chapter Eight

Isabel

Two weeks later

It was insane how fast those last two weeks went by, but here I was, standing near the moving truck, my heart breaking, but my strength doubling. I wouldn't cry, not in front of my parents, and especially not in front of Quinn.

The last fourteen days had been hectic as we packed, with movers coming in and out of the house to help load the truck. Everything within these last fourteen days had been a blur.

What I do remember is the time I spent with Quinn. Those stolen moments at school where he'd pull me into a darkened corner and kiss me until I was breathless. It was the memories of the way he'd hold my hand, tracing my fingers with one of his as we lay on the couch, a movie playing in the background that neither of us focused on. It didn't take long for the school to find out we weren't just friends any longer, although I'd been surprised at how many of our friends had seen this moment coming.

And then we'd told my parents we loved each other, and that after school there wouldn't be anything keeping us apart. They hadn't seemed shocked.

Neither had Quinn's parents.

"I'll come with you. I'll find a way to work it all out."

I closed my eyes and played the words Quinn said to me last night over and over in my head.

"I'd go with you to the end of the world if it meant we'd always be together."

God, he was like ... not real.

I could have laughed at my thoughts, but it was the truth. I was lucky, that was for sure, because a relationship like we had was timeless.

"Hey," he said as he came up to stand beside me.

I turned my head and looked up at him. "Hi." My throat was tight, emotion threatening to make itself known. He wrapped his arm around me and pulled me close. Since confessing we loved each other we'd spent every day together.

He'd see me first thing in the morning, all day at school, and he'd spend the evening with me, only leaving when my father forced him to leave because it was late. And then there were those times we'd sneak away and be alone, and I'd give myself to him over and over again, just holding him and wanting those moments to last forever.

"It'll be okay."

I nodded, because although it seemed impossible right now, I knew things would work out. But what gutted me was the fact I was moving so far away, and that it wasn't like either of us, or even our families, had funds to fly either of us out every weekend, especially during the school year.

Believe me, we'd tried to work it out. But in the end, we both knew it couldn't happen. We needed to finish school if we wanted to have any kind of productive life together. If Quinn left school to move out west with me, where would we be in the end?

Love was everything, but I couldn't let him ruin his future because I was moping around and he hated to see me upset.

"No crying, okay?" he said and turned me around, cupped my cheek, and leaned down to kiss me. I melted into him, not caring if the movers, neighbors, or even my parent's saw. Let them gawk at us, let them feel uncomfortable that Quinn held me close, that he kissed me like he was starving, and I was the only person that could sate his appetite.

I heard the moving truck door slide shut; the loud whoosh and click caused reality to set in. I pulled back, not wanting to, but also knowing I couldn't hold on to this moment forever.

But I want to. I desperately want to.

"It's time to go, Isabel," my dad said, but I didn't look at him.

Quinn smiled down at me, stroked my cheek with his thumb, and I leaned into his touch.

"It'll work out," Quinn said again.

I sure hoped so.

Quinn

As soon as I couldn't see the moving van, I got in my car and headed to the mechanic shop where I worked. For the last couple of weeks, since I found out Isabel was leaving, I'd been putting things in order, trying to work things out in between seeing her. I wanted to spend as much time as I could with her, but I also had a lot of shit to do in a short amount of time.

I'd told Isabel we could make the long distance relationship work, and I would in a heartbeat, but if there was anything I could do to make it work being with her and lessen that year timeframe, I was going to try.

I pulled the car into the shop, cut the engine, got out, and headed to Brae's office. I knocked three times before hearing the manager shout out. "Unless you have food, fuck off."

I pushed the door open anyway and saw Brae hunched over his desk, papers strewn everywhere. He snapped his head up, the scowl on his face aimed at me. But when he recognized me, he straightened and leaned back.

"You have food?"

I shook my head. "Does it look like it?"

Brae scowled harder and then chuckled. "Then what the fuck you want, boy?"

"You hear anything new from your friend out west?" I held my breath. This was going to make it a hell of a lot easier for me to go early and be with Isabel.

But there wasn't anything that would keep me from her, not even shit that didn't go my way.

I wasn't waiting a fucking year to be with my girl.

"Yeah, I heard from him."

I waited, the silence stretching. Finally I lifted my eyebrow, growing impatient. "And? Does he have anything out there for me?"

"You sure you want to do this?"

"Yeah, I'm really fucking sure." There was no doubt in my mind what I wanted and that was Isabel.

"What about school?" Brae asked. "You leaving without graduating is really fucking stupid, Quinn."

I shook my head. "I talked with the school, crammed my credits, and can graduate early." I was pretty good in school, but I hadn't worried about trying to graduate early because what would be the point? The girl I loved would still be going, and I wanted to be with her.

But, thank fuck, I'd had extra credits and could get out early, but it would take a couple of months for everything to play into motion and fall where it needed to. But a couple of months was a hell of a lot better than a year.

I also didn't give a shit about graduating with my class.

I meant it when I said Isabel was my life, and I'd do anything to be with her.

Brae didn't speak for several long seconds. He exhaled finally, reached over, and opened one of his desk drawers. He pulled a slip of paper out and handed it over.

I grabbed it and looked down at the name, address, and number jotted down.

"Mitchell can hook you up with steady work as well as room and board."

I folded up the paper and looked back up at Brae.

"Don't fuck this up, though. I vouched for you," Brae said.

"You know I won't. Thank you for doing this for me, man."

"You tell her you put all of this together?"

I shook my head. "I didn't want to say anything in case shit fell through."

Brae nodded. "She must be something special for you to jump through hoops like this."

I didn't even have to think of a response, because I knew the lengths I'd go for Isabel, to be with her.

"She's my everything."

Chapter Nine

Isabel

A month later

I spoke with Quinn every day, but that didn't make this separation any easier. What really sucked was the fact we hadn't been able to travel to each other since I moved across the country, and it felt like I'd left a little part of myself back home.

Home. That's where Quinn was.

That's where I was supposed to be, where I was meant to be.

I stared out the window of the library, a place I had started going to shortly after we moved to this new city because I wanted to have a little bit of quiet. But the silence just had me thinking about Quinn.

Who am I kidding? I think of Quinn every second of every day.

I stared down at my textbook. It was a Friday night, and here I was, sitting in the library, studying for a test I didn't have for another week. But I had no interest in hanging out with the friend I'd made, and I had no desire to hang out at home and watch reruns with my mother either.

I was happy for my parents, though; glad they could finally own that really nice house they'd always wanted. I was happy my dad got the promotion he so deserved, and that all those years of busting his ass had paid off.

But I was depressed, and no amount of talking to Quinn, even if it was several times a day, could help that.

I just needed to be with him.

He was my soul mate, my other half, and not having him by my side was torture. For so long we'd been together, talking, laughing, hell, just staring at the stars in that cornfield as the silence stretched on. If two people were meant to be together, it was he and I.

I lifted my phone and hit the calendar app, staring at the days I'd already marked off before I could see him again. I was about to set my phone down when it started vibrating. Looking around to make sure I wouldn't disrupt anyone, I saw I was alone and answered my cell.

"Hi," I said softly, the smile covering my face instantly.

"Hey, baby." Quinn's deep voice always sent shivers through me. "What are you doing?"

I looked down at my textbook and pushed it away. "Thinking of you."

His deep chuckle had my body heating in the best of ways.

"I'm always thinking about you, Isabel."

God, I loved to hear him say those kinds of things, words that were sweet and endearing, but that also made me wish I could fall into his powerful embrace. "I wish you were here right now," I found myself saying, even though I'd told myself I wouldn't do that to him, wouldn't make this situation any more difficult.

It was hard enough on both of us.

Quinn

For the last month, there wasn't anything I wanted more than to tell Isabel I wasn't letting her go without a fight ... that I'd be with her soon. A year was far too long to be apart from her, even if we could have found a way to see each other during that time. I needed her by my side, an arm's length reach from me.

Obsessive.

Possessive.

Territorial.

I was all of those things and more when it came to Isabel.

I'd gone to her house first. Her mother had been surprised, of course, and as much as I would have liked to speak to her more, catch up, I was here because of Isabel.

I'd come to be with my girl.

Here I was behind a bookshelf, staring at the person that meant the world to me, and having to use a lot of self-control not to just go to her. But as I took that first step, I watched her stand and pack up her stuff. I asked her about her day, just wanting to hear her voice.

"And no fuckers going after you?" I asked, tracking her movements through the library. She laughed, but I was being serious. I could admit I was one jealous motherfucker when it came to Isabel.

"No, of course not. I don't give anyone the time of day." She stepped out of the library and made her way to her car. I'd parked right next to her, the back of my car crammed with boxes, and a small trailer that held the rest of my meager possessions. Since Brae had gotten me a job here with a guy he worked with, and it included room and board, I would be able to save up for a place for my girl and me when she was finished with school.

"I miss you," I said and followed her to her car, staying behind enough that she couldn't hear me talking to her, not just yet anyway. She exhaled, and I could see from her profile that she looked so damn sad.

"Me too." But then she stopped at the trunk of her car, staring at my vehicle. I could see the realization, the confusion, and finally, the shock filter across her face. I was a few feet behind her now, waiting for her to turn around and see me. Standing still and not pulling her close was hard as fuck.

"Quinn?" she whispered and finally turned around. We locked stares, and the phone fell from her hand, clattering to the ground.

I didn't think about anything else but shoving my cell in my pocket and heading for her. I pulled her close to me, cupped the back of her head, and whispered in her ear. "I'm here, and I'm not going anywhere."

"I don't understand," she whispered, and I could hear her crying. She pulled away, and I smiled down at her. I brushed away a tear with my thumb, then leaned down to kiss the other side of her face, brushing my lips over the salty wetness.

"I told you everything would be okay, that I'd make everything work out."

"But school, money? And what about your parents? They were okay—"

I kissed her, stopping her from saying anything else. After several seconds, and when I knew she was good and breathless for me, I pulled away. "I had enough credits to graduate early, and I've been working toward being able to come out here with a job and place to stay." I cupped her cheek and stared into her eyes.

"And my mom and dad know how much I love you. They know there isn't anything I wouldn't do to be with you." I stroked her cheek. "Nothing could keep me from you."

"You did all of that for me?" she asked with wonder in her voice.

I shook my head. "Isabel, there isn't anything on this fucking planet I wouldn't do for you." I leaned in close, so we were eye to eye. "There isn't anything I wouldn't do for us."

"God, how did I get so lucky?" She was crying again, and I smiled.

"I'm the lucky one." And I was. God, I was so fucking lucky to have her in my life, to have her as mine.

Epilogue

Isabel

Two years later

The last two years had been hard financially and with both of our schedules. Since Quinn had shown up and surprised me, dropped his life behind to come to me, we'd made it work.

There was nothing else we wanted more.

After I graduated high school, I'd decided to stay. Since Quinn had uprooted his life to be with me, I'd applied at a community college in town. It didn't matter where I went to school, as long as we were together. Besides, I told myself I could get all of my core classes done anywhere.

But after being here for two years, and now done with all my prerequisite classes, I'd applied to the local collage. Quinn was taking classes as well, slowly, but he was getting his business degree to help manage the construction business Mitchell owned; the guy had given him a job and place to stay when he moved out here.

I closed my book and got up off the couch, hearing the lawnmower cut off. Our house was a one-room rental, and although it was small, it beat the hell out of living with Mitch or with my parents.

Leaning against the window, I pulled the curtain aside and saw Quinn bent over the lawnmower, messing with something on it. He was shirtless, his big body even more muscular since working construction. Sweat gleamed off his body, and as if we hadn't been a couple for the last two years and had enough sex to last us a lifetime, my body instantly reacted.

I grew wet and needy, my body wanting the thing only Quinn could give me.

He turned then, lifted his arm, and wiped the sweat off his forehead with his forearm. I watched the play of muscles moving along his arm, at the way the sinew flexed under the golden skin, at the way power came off him like another entity.

And then he turned and looked at me, and all I could see was us naked, and his very sweaty body pressed against mine.

He came toward the house, pulled the door open, and went into the kitchen. I heard the water turn on and a second later it kicked off. When he came back to where I stood, he was drying his hands off, the pleasure on his face instant as he looked me up and down.

I knew what was coming. I anticipated it. We were only feet apart now, both of us breathing heavily, the arousal moving between us. It was as if, as the seconds ticked by, the arousal bounced between us, growing, becoming this raging inferno.

"I want you," he said in a scratchy voice.

I lowered my gaze and saw how hard he was for me. "I can see you do." He made this low sound in his throat, and God, did that turn me on. I watched beads of sweat trail down his hard, tattooed body, and every erogenous zone in me heightened, came alive, and screamed out to give in.

I could smell him from where I stood, all clean male sweat and need for me. He came closer then, his head lowered, his eyes focused on me. I backed away, knowing he liked the chase, that he liked me to play hard to get. When the wall stopped me, he leaned his face in close to me.

"You feel what you do to me?" He pressed his erection into my belly, and I shamelessly moaned at the feeling. It felt like he was hiding a steel pipe between his legs. Another gush of wetness slipped out of me, and I shifted, trying to get closer.

His mouth was so close to mine that I just wanted to lean in and kiss him. But I liked having him take control.

He kept his eyes trained right at me, but instead of kissing me like I desperately wanted, he dragged his lips along my cheek. Not able to hold my eyes open at the feeling, I let my head fall back against the door.

He ground his dick into me again, over and over, until I found myself reaching up and holding onto his biceps for support. He was rock hard and tense beneath my palms, and I slid my hands over the bulging definition of his arms.

"If you want me," I whispered, "take me."

"Fuck. You can't say that shit, or I'll come right in my jeans."

He moved his lips along the shell of my ear, and a shiver worked through me. He groaned and pressed his entire length against me, making me see and feel that he was ready for me.

"No one will ever compare to you." His tongue continued along the shell of my ear, and I moaned. He pulled away only enough that he had his mouth close to mine once more. "You smell so fucking good," he growled.

Then his mouth was on mine, and was running his tongue along my bottom lip. I heard his nails dig into the door. I opened my mouth, took his tongue between my lips, and sucked on it. He tasted spicy, yet sweet: salty, yet masculine.

"I don't want slow," I moaned.

"Good, because I wasn't going to give it to you that way."

Quinn

I was so fucking hard I could have driven nails through steel.

My cock throbbed, and all I wanted to do was lose it with her. A groan left me at the image that thought conjured up. I didn't break our kiss as I reached between us with one hand and all but tore the button from her pants, ripped the zipper down, and tried to push the material down her legs. Fuck, I needed her naked now.

Isabel was hot and sweet and surrendering herself to me. She knew I needed her, and her body was primed for me. When she put her hands on my chest and pushed me away, taking a step back was a really hard fucking thing to do. But she wasn't stopping this, I could tell. No, we were just getting started.

Isabel removed her pants, shirt, and her bra in record time; I reached down and palmed my cock through my jeans. I all but ripped my button off, pulled the zipper down, and got out of my jeans. Maybe I should have showered first, but the thought of having her like this, dirty and raw, turned me the fuck on.

I slipped my thumbs under the edge of her panties and pushed them down her legs. Fuck, the material was soaking wet, and it was all because of me.

I could have come just listening to her rapid breathing, because I knew she was panting like that because she was so turned on.

I looked down at her pussy. That trimmed triangle of hair covering her cunt drove me wild, and I made this low sound of need. Possessive need slammed into me, and I knew this would be a fast, hard fuck.

I looked at her tits, those perfect C-cups that had pre-cum slipping out of the slit on my cock. I could imagine my cum all over those glorious globes.

There was a lot of dirty shit I wanted to do to her right now, but before I could even move, she got down on her knees and had my cock in her hand.

"Fuck," I whispered harshly.

My fucking cock pointed right at her mouth, and fortunately she didn't tease me, because I didn't have the control to handle that right now.

She tightened her palm around my shaft, and this strangled noise left me. I slammed my hand on the wall in front of me when she took the head into the hot, wet confines of her suctioning mouth. I couldn't help closing my eyes as she started to mouth fuck me.

"That's it, baby. That's so fucking it."

She took as much as she could, hollowed out her cheeks, and relaxed her throat.

"Oh. Yeah."

Isabel made a humming noise around me and I groaned, curling my hand into a fist on the wall, praying I didn't shoot my load in her mouth. I wanted my cock deep in her cunt when I did that.

And then she deep throated me, and I nearly lost it. The head of my cock nudged the back of her throat, but she didn't give up. She reached down, took my balls in one hand, and gave them a squeeze that bordered on pain.

"Fucking hell. Yes, Isabel." I had to stop her or I'd come, and I didn't want it to end like this. I wanted her coming for me first. I helped her to her feet, grabbed her chin with my hand, and tilted her head back. Then I kissed her until she was clinging to me, as if she couldn't stand on her own.

I pulled away and looked down at her mouth. Her lips were swollen and red, and a surge of proprietary need slammed into me, knowing *I'd* made them look like that. I slammed my mouth on hers again.

Moving one of my hands down her back and over the generous mounds of her ass, I groaned when I felt the nice, full weight under my palm. I squeezed the globe and dug my fingers into the warm, soft flesh.

"You've got a fucking juicy ass, Isabel." I licked at the inside of her mouth. I gave her ass cheek a swat and loved when she breathed out roughly. "You like when I have my dick all up in you back here?" She didn't answer verbally, just nodded. "Yeah, you do." I kissed her harder. "You like when I'm stretching you, making you feel so full you feel like you might split in two?"

"God, yes, Quinn."

I growled low in approval.

"Harder," she breathed, and I squeezed her ass cheek with more force.

"There will be bruises come morning if I go much harder," I gritted out, wanting to go so fucking hard, but also not wanting to hurt her.

"Good," she breathed out against my mouth. "You know I want your mark on me."

Christ.

My girl was a freak, and I fucking loved it.

I was rougher, harder, smacking her ass cheek, digging my fingers into her flesh until she gasped and shook for me.

I ran my tongue over the underside of her jaw, licking her flesh, tasting the salty sweetness that covered her. When I got to her ear, I ran my tongue over the shell, loving how she shivered for me and dug her nails into my biceps. "I want to be inside you right now," I said on a harsh groan.

"I want you inside me, Quinn."

Using my other hand, I gripped her behind one knee and lifted her leg up to wrap it around my waist. If she wanted my cock in her, I'd give her every thick, long inch.

I reached between our bodies, took hold of my cock and started rubbing the head of my dick up and down her slit. My cock head was getting nice and wet from her cream, and I had to clench my jaw to try and hold off from shooting my load on her.

Without anymore waiting, I grabbed her ass with my other hand, lifted her slight weight easily, and grunted when she wrapped her other leg around my waist. She was so spread for me, her cunt warm, wet, and my cock right between her folds, absorbing it all.

She dug her heels into the small of my back, and I reached between us to position my dick head at her pussy hole. Burying my face in the crook of her neck, I surged into her body, a harsh bark leaving me at how tight and hot she was.

I'd never get enough of this, never get enough of how good she felt.

I pounded into her, thrusting my cock deep in her, wanting to feel my tip hit her cervix, wanting my cum shooting right up in her and getting her pregnant.

God, the very thought of her big with my baby had me nearly busting a nut right here.

"Oh yeah. Fuck, Isabel." I pounded into her, knowing I was being too rough but not able to help myself. She held on, licked at my ear, ran her teeth along the flesh, and my whole body shook for her.

Up against the wall sex was hot, but she needed to be in our bed beneath me as I fucked the hell out of her.

Holding her tight and making sure my cock stayed right in her cunt, I turned and made my way toward our room. I kicked the bedroom door open and it slammed against the wall, the picture hanging beside it rattling from the force. I had her in the center of the bed a second later, my body blanketing her, and I started thrusting like a madman. I held her legs open and watched my cock sink in and out of her, her pussy stretched white, the skin pink, soaked.

Sliding my hands down the inside of her thighs. I framed her pussy and placed my thumbs right by her cunt hole. I pulled the skin out slightly, and a moan left her.

"More," she cried out, her pussy clenching around me.

"You want more?" I ground out.

"Yes," she said in a rush, her head now tilted back, her eyes closed and her mouth parted.

I placed my thumb on the hard little nub at the top of her pussy and rubbed the fuck out of it, wanting her coming for me. She writhed on the bed and started lifting her hips to meet my thrusts. The sloppy sound of her wet pussy sucking at my cock filled the room, made me drunk, frenzied. The sweet, musky smell of her pussy rose up like an undercut to my jaw.

God, it was so fucking hot.

"Come on, baby. I want you to come for me."

"Oh," she whispered, and her pussy milked my shaft.

And like a good girl, she was coming for me.

The rhythmic pull of her inner muscles milking my dick would have sent me over the edge, but I wasn't ready to have this end yet. When her tremors subsided, I forced myself to pull out. I wanted my face buried in her cunt, wanted her cream covering my mouth, her juices down my throat. I wanted her to get off with my tongue and lips.

"Get on your belly and pop your ass out for me."

She was on her belly a second later, and I grabbed her hips and lifted the bottom of her body up. Her cheeks spread, and I saw an unobstructed view of her asshole.

Gorgeous.

Her pussy was spread, too, all juicy looking, all pink and swollen from the fucking I'd given her. I wanted to see my cum slipping out of her and dripping down her inner thighs. I moved lower and onto my belly so my face was right up in her cunt. She smelled so damn good.

"I'm going to devour you."

I ate her out, licked her from pussy hole to clit, right up her center.

Over and over I did this, sucking at her like she was an ice cream cone. I shoved my tongue into her cunt and fucked her with the muscle, feeling her clench around me. She started grinding herself on my mouth, breathing hard and sounding sexy as hell.

"That's it. Fuck yourself on me."

"Yes. God, Quinn." Her words were muffled against the bed, but I didn't stop licking her to answer. I flattened my tongue and moved it to her clit, sucking that hard little nub in my mouth. I loved the wet suctioning sound that filled my head, and I got off on the way she thrust herself back at me.

I started dry humping the fuck out of the mattress, trying to ease the ache in my shaft and balls. I wanted to see her get off for me, so I sucked her clit furiously, humming around it, knowing she was close.

"Come on, Isabel. Come for me," I murmured against her soaked, hot flesh.

"*Oh*," she whispered. She lifted up her ass a little more, and a tremor worked over her entire body as she came for me. Yeah, that's what I was talking about ... her surrender. I loved the way her pussy hole clenched, as if it needed my big cock inside of it.

Finally, when her orgasm faded, I took hold of the root of my cock, stroked the fucker a few times, and stared right at her pussy hole, wanting to be deep in that warmth right now. "Get on your back for me, baby girl." She obeyed instantly, her tits shaking slightly from the act.

I didn't waste any time getting between her splayed thighs. I positioned my cockhead at her pussy again and stared into her eyes. Without thinking or talking, I pushed into her, just shoved my cock deep in her body.

"God," she moaned and closed her eyes.

I was buried in her wet heat, not able to go slow. I needed her like I needed to fucking breathe.

"Fuck me," she whispered.

"*Christ.*"

I did just that.

I pounded into her, pulling my cock out before slamming it back in. Her tits bounced from the fierce motion, and I was riveted to the sight. Slowly I lifted my gaze from her tits to her face and felt this low growl leave me at the look of ecstasy on her face.

She opened her eyes and stared at me. "I'm going to come." She arched her back, her tits thrust out. I leaned down and ran my tongue along the underside of her throat, loving the saltiness on her skin. I felt her pussy clench around my dick, and couldn't stop from going over the edge.

I was gong to fill her up with my jizz, make it slide out of her when I pulled out.

I wanted the sheets wet underneath her.

I wanted to put so much of my seed in her that tomorrow when she sat down, it would still be coming out of her, making her panties wet.

And then I felt my orgasm approach. It was a tightening in my back, a tingling in my balls. It moved quickly through me, and I fucking let it.

"God, yes." I rested my face in the crook of her neck and let myself go over the edge just as she cried out in pleasure. And when my orgasm rushed out, my cum filling her, I roared out how much I loved her.

Isabel was mine.

My cum in her, on her skin, was me marking her.

When I couldn't hold myself up anymore, I rolled off her, not wanting to crush her. But I put my hand right between her thighs, rose up on my elbow, and looked down at her.

"This is mine," I said and added a little bit of pressure between her thighs. She made the sweetest gasp. I felt her wetness and my cum start sliding out of her. I wanted it in her. I wanted it staying where it belonged. I leaned in close, feeling her breath along my lips. "And when I had my cock in you for the first time, Isabel, that was me owning you."

She closed her eyes and hummed, and I felt like a bastard for saying this shit to her, but I couldn't help myself.

"Have I told you how much I like having you all possessive and growly with me?" She opened her eyes and smiled up at me. I leaned down and kissed her.

"I'm glad you like me like this, because with you, I feel pretty fucking territorial."

She rolled onto her side, curled against me, and I held her. I lifted her hand and looked at the engagement ring I'd given her just last month. I should have proposed long ago, but I wanted to give her time to settle in, to start school, to find her way. But truth is I would have married her as soon as I knew she loved me back all those years ago. I didn't care if we were young, or if our parents might not have approved.

Isabel was the very reason I breathed.

"I should shower, baby." I pulled away, knowing she probably didn't like my sweatiness covering her, but she held onto me and snuggled in deeper.

"Just hold me."

I wrapped my arms around Isabel and did just that. I certainly didn't deserve her, but I had her, and I was going to make sure she knew exactly how much she meant to me each and every fucking day.

The End

BABY FEVER

A Real Man, 3

BABY FEVER (A Real Man, 3)
By Jenika Snow
www.JenikaSnow.com
Jenika_Snow@Yahoo.com
Copyright © August 2016 by Jenika Snow
First E-book Publication: August 2016
Photographer: Wander Aguiar :: Photography
Cover model: Jacob Hogue
Photo provided by: Wander Book Club

He's done being the bad boy ... he's ready to be a father.

Dex

I'm the bad boy— the one mothers warn their daughters about. But I've never seen myself settling down, and that's been fine with me. Then life, reality, whatever you want to call it, bitch slapped me right across the face, and I knew what I wanted.

A baby.

At thirty-nine, I am having a severe case of baby fever, and that means convincing the one woman I've always wanted but knew was too good for me to be mine and be the mother of my child.

Eva

I've always wanted Dex. It's hard not to want a man like Dex. He's all raw power and cut muscle. He's the epitome of what a real man is, but he's not a bastard about it.

But then he throws me a curve ball and says he wants me not only as his woman ... but as the mother of his child.

And I'll be honest; it's what I've always wanted.

Dex

The truth is Eva deserves better than me, but I'm too selfish, and I want her too badly to back away.

Nothing will stop me from making her mine ... and putting my baby inside her.

Warning: This book is short and right to the point—like the kind of story that gives you whiplash. If you enjoy

unbelievable plots, and insta-everything going on, you may enjoy this dirty little read.

USA Today Bestselling Author
Jenika Snow

He's going to put
his baby in her...

Baby
FEVER

A Real Man

Chapter One

Dex

I had a severe case of baby fever going on, and I knew exactly which woman I wanted to help me get what I needed.

Eva.

Fucking Eva with her lush curves and hips that are wide and meant to carry my child. I could come just looking at her.

All I could think about was breeding with her, filling her with my spunk, and making her mine.

And she would be mine.

I nearly groaned at the thought of having her, of her being mine.

I'd known her for years, but she was too good for me, too sweet.

But I was also too fucking selfish to let her get away.

I had a reputation for getting into trouble and starting fights with assholes that looked at me the wrong way.

What I didn't have a reputation for was being a womanizer. I was picky as fuck with the females I let into my bed. But they were also empty fucks, a night of release because I was wound up.

What I wanted with Eva was more than just a few hours between the sheets, but I didn't even know if she'd give me the time of day.

She never had before, and a part of me wanted her even more because of it. My bad boy reputation didn't make her a clinger, and she sure as fuck didn't present herself to me like an animal in heat.

Yeah, she would be mine.

I reached down and adjusted my cock. It was rock hard and pressed against the zipper of my jeans.

I focused on Eva again, watching her get the drink order from the bar, and then she made her way toward the table. The bar I was in, and the one she worked at, was the only decent hangout place in this town. But I didn't give a shit about hanging out or getting drunk. I came here to see her.

I finished off the last of my beer, set the bottle aside, and didn't care if I was being obvious in checking out Eva.

"Another one?" Jarren, the owner of the bar and a good friend, asked as he took the empty beer bottle off the table.

"Nah, I'm good," I said, my focus still on Eva. "Wait," I ended up saying to Jarren. "Yeah, I'll take another." It would give me an excuse to loiter here and check out Eva. I also needed to figure out how in the hell I was going to make her mine.

If Eva knew what I was thinking right now, how I wanted to lift up that skirt of hers, pull her panties aside, and plunge my dick in her, she'd probably think I was a sick fuck. But hell, I wanted to do more than that. I wanted to go raw inside her, fill her with my cum, and put my baby in her belly.

I wanted to breed with her like I was some kind of fucking animal. I wanted her to grow big with my child, and just thinking about getting her pregnant made me hard.

I was so damn hard.

I was ready to settle down with the one woman I'd never gone after for fear of shit getting weird between her brother and me.

But fuck that. I was older and knew what I wanted. I wanted Eva as mine.

Only mine.

Eva

I could feel his eyes on me. It was like fingers skating down my spine. To say I was affected was an understatement.

I wanted Dex. I always have.

To say I didn't get wet because of his bad boy attitude, his hard demeanor, or the fact I knew he liked to skate with trouble back in the day, would have been a bold faced lie.

He'd been a friend of my brother, Charlie, for years. I didn't think Charlie would give a shit if I had something going on with his friend, but Dex has never really seen me as anything more than Charlie's little sister. At least, I never felt like he did.

Although for a while now, I'd seen the way he watched me: with this intensity in his eyes that set me on edge and made me question my good intentions.

What good intentions? You've wanted Dex to fuck you for so long you can't even be next to him without getting wet.

"Hey, you with us or what, Sugar?" Jarren asked.

I glanced at my boss, trying to clear my head. "I'm fine," I said and cleared my throat.

"Well, you want to take this beer over to Dex?"

I licked my lips and nodded. The hairs on the back of my neck stood on end, and I glanced over my shoulder to see the man I'd been fantasizing about for far too long staring right at me. He sat in one of the corner tables, the shadows partially concealing him.

A tingle worked its way up my spine.

I grabbed the beer bottle, as well as a few mixed drinks I had to drop off at another table. It would have been smarter for me to give Dex his beer first, that way I had an excuse to leave, but I dropped off the mixed drinks first and made my way over to Dex.

He leaned back, one leg kicked out, his arm thrown over the back of his chair. He had his other arm on the table, his tattooed flesh instantly arousing me.

Who are you kidding? You're perpetually aroused around him.

Taking a steadying breath, I smiled and handed him the beer. But before I could turn and leave, he reached out and took hold of my wrist. I looked down, my throat tight, my heart racing. Even his hands were tattooed, a fact I found so damn hot.

"What's up?" I managed to say, but my voice sounded strained. Some classic rock song was playing from the old as hell jukebox in the corner, and I could make out through my peripheral vision a couple nearly dry humping on the dance floor. But my eyes were trained on Dex, because hell if I could look away.

"What time do you get off?" he asked, and for a second, my heart stopped. I lowered my brows.

"Ten, why?" I managed to tug my arm free, not because I wanted him to stop touching me, but because I was worried he'd feel my hand shaking. I clenched my fingers inward, my nails digging into my palm.

He shrugged his broad shoulders and leaned forward, placing his forearms on the scarred round table. "We haven't caught up, Eva."

A shiver worked its way up my spine at the sound of my name on his lips.

"What's there to catch up with, Dex?" I was starting to sweat.

Truth was this was probably the most interest he'd taken in me in ... forever. Sure, he was nice to me, but it was as if he saw me as nothing more than Charlie's little sister. He didn't see me as a friend he wanted to hang out with, and certainly not someone he'd take to his bed.

"Plenty," he said and lifted the corner of his mouth. "How about we hang out after work? Catch-up and all that shit, Eva girl?"

God, he was so handsome. The tattoos were just the icing on the manly cake that made up Dex. I also knew he had both nipples pierced, and I'd heard him talking to Charlie back in the day about getting his dick pierced. Whether the latter was true or not was not something I would probably ever find out.

And then there was his hair, slightly longer and hanging down to his chin when he didn't put it up in a manbun.

You want to stand here and appraise him? God, you probably look like a weirdo not responding.

I swallowed again as memories played through my head.

"Catch up?" I asked.

He nodded and gave me a sexy full-blown grin.

"Maybe the three of us could all hang out? I know Charlie said it's been a while since you guys saw each other." I don't know why I was trying to get my brother in on this, because I did want to hang out with Dex. And being alone with him didn't sound too bad either.

He leaned back again and shook his head, but didn't respond right away. Instead, I saw him looking me up and down. I could have played it off like nothing, but that was not an innocent look.

No, he was eye fucking me.

"I don't think Charlie needs to hang with us. I mean, I have seen him plenty of times. You and I need to rekindle shit, Eva. A little alone time sounds good, right?"

I found myself nodding.

And then I was thinking about the past again.

When he used to come over to hang out with Charlie, they would stay in the garage, working on Charlie's car, drinking beer when our dad wasn't watching, and talking about "pussy." Ten years older than me, I was the stereotypical annoying sister, but as the years passed, my attraction for Dex grew.

It was that age-old trope about the younger woman wanting her older brother's friend.

Yet, I never got the guy.

Now I was hitting twenty-nine, wasn't married, and had no kids; I was in a damn rut.

The truth was there were plenty of times I'd gone for runs in town, or just gone shopping and I'd see families, mothers with their children, newborns crying, babies giggling, and ache to have that in my life.

I was twenty-nine years old, for God's sake, and not getting any younger. My biological clock was ticking, and I wanted to be a mother.

But I didn't want to get knocked up just for the sake of being a mother, and certainly not by some guy I'd just met.

"You want to hang with me, Eva, spend some time together?" His voice was low, coaxing even. "How about I hear you say it?" The rough timbre had this shiver skating up my spine.

No, there was one person I'd always wanted—secretly loved, too—but I knew being anything with Dex was never going to happen.

I knew damn well I was never going to be his. I would never have gorgeous babies with him ... and damn, would his babies be beautiful.

I tried to clear my thoughts, but yeah, it was no use, especially not when he was right in front of me.

I thought about how Dex acted all interested in me. As much as I wanted to play it cool and act like it didn't affect me ... it sure as hell did.

"Yes, I want to spend some time with you." There, I said it. It felt good to admit it, actually.

"Good. That's real good, Eva." He grinned again. "I'll be waiting for you outside when you get off."

I felt my cheeks heat as I thought of all kinds of dirty things when he said "Get off."

For some reason, this felt like I was playing with fire, but hell, I didn't mind getting burned.

Chapter Two

Dex

I'd just gone all in here, and I didn't know how in the fuck I was going to get Eva to agree to be mine and have my baby. I wanted her like a fiend, and I sure as hell knew she wanted me. She kept zoning in and out there when we were talking, and I wondered if she was thinking dirty shit about me ... like I was of her.

I leaned back against my sixty-nine Mustang, my arms crossed over my chest, and my focus on the two drunken assholes standing by the front entrance. They were loud and obnoxious as fuck, and hearing the lewd comments they were tossing out at the women who were leaving was starting to piss me off.

I might have a reputation in town as being a bad boy, and gotten into plenty of trouble when I was younger, but I sure as fuck didn't disrespect women.

And then there she was, her focus on her purse as she rummaged through it. I was about to push off the car and walk toward her, but I froze, every muscle in my body tightening when one of the drunken fuckers approached her.

"Hey, baby. You served me drinks tonight, remember?"

"Unfortunately, I do." She didn't even look up as she responded.

I had to smile. My girl was hard as nails and didn't take any shit when the time called for it.

"Hey, you're acting like a little bi—"

She lifted her head then, and the guy stopped speaking. If her stare could kill a man, he would have been in the ground already. "Watch it, asshole."

I could have let her handle it, but the truth was I wanted to be the man that stepped in and took care of his woman.

And she will be my woman.

But, even if I *didn't* want her as mine, I wouldn't have let any bastard speak to a woman like that. I moved toward the pricks, and just when the asshole opened his mouth again, I pulled Eva back behind me. She made this small sound, maybe from shock, or maybe in protest. I didn't care at the moment, though. I was in fight mode; whether it actually came down to that or not remained to be seen.

"What were you about to say to my woman?" I said through clenched teeth. The fuckers reeked of alcohol, and as they cocked their heads back to look into my face, I couldn't help but feel that predatory sense rise up in me.

They wouldn't push this. They might be drunk, might even be fuckers, but they were in flight mode. I could see it in their eyes. It was that fear, that realization they'd get their asses kicked to next week if they pushed this.

"Whatever," the asshole muttered, and he let his friend take him away. I watched them until they disappeared down the street and then finally turned around and looked at Eva. I couldn't help but grin at the death stare she was giving me.

"I had it under control," she said, and I nodded.

"I know, but I couldn't let a prick shit on you like that. It wouldn't be very gentlemanly of me." I saw the fight drain out of her, and she loosened up a bit.

"Thanks."

I nodded again, feeling pretty fucking proud at her words. Hearing her say that one word made me feel like a real man. I might have only stood up for her, but I would have laid it down to the pavement if it came down to that.

She stared at me for a second, and I saw her start to get nervous. It was a shift in the way she stood, a flutter of her eyes, and the fact she was picking at the strap of her purse, not really realizing it.

"Okay, well, I'll see you around?" She made it sound like a question, even though she knew damn well I wanted to talk with her.

I reached out and grabbed her wrist. God, that spark of electricity was instant and traveled right up my arms. She looked over at me, and our eyes locked.

"I want to talk with you, catch up." I still held her wrist in a loose but solid hold. "Come for a ride with me?" I asked it as a question, but I wouldn't take no for an answer. I wanted her too badly, and I'd made up my mind about what I wanted; I wasn't backing off.

"And where exactly do you want to go?" She lifted an eyebrow, her emotions clear on her face.

I couldn't help but grin, thinking I'd like her in my bed, under me, and filled with my cum. Of course, I wasn't about to go there … yet. "Anywhere. You can pick. I just want to talk, see how things have been with you."

She looked a bit hesitant, and although I still held her wrist gently in my grasp, I wanted to pull her closer so she slammed into me, so I could feel the womanly curves that made up her body.

"It's late."

"It is." I thought she was going to turn me down, which I'd have to retaliate by insisting we hang out. I'd wanted this for a while, but I guess I just needed some kind of internal kick in the ass to get things going. "But you did admit you wanted to hang out." I grinned.

I was glad I was finally facing my reality and not being a douche and trying to ignore it.

She laughed softly. "Okay, Dex."

I felt her pulse beating rapidly beneath my thumb, and I started stroking her flesh, feeling it increase in speed with each passing caress.

She was so fucking into this, even if she tried to act all nonchalant and shit.

"But how about you follow me? It'll be easier that way. We can go to the lake."

Charlie and I used to go to the lake to get drunk and smoke a little pot way back in the day. Once Eva was sixteen, she'd tagged along with us a few times, sneaking some sips of beer from Charlie's bottle.

Oh yeah, seclusion, a little quiet.

That's exactly what I was fucking talking about.

"Sounds good," I said, acting cool, like I wasn't really fucking looking forward to this. Hell, I wasn't about to fuck Eva tonight, even if my dick got hard just looking at her. But having some alone time with her, working up to getting to where I wanted with her, was a good start.

I finally let go of her wrist and dragged my thumb along her pulse point.

"Lead the way." I grinned. Yeah, this was really fucking good.

Chapter Three

Eva

I sat on the hood of Dex's Mustang, looking over at the lake and wondering what was really going on. I'd seen Dex around town, and although we'd drifted apart as the years passed, we'd always remained friends. Not like how he was with Charlie, but that was a given since the two of them spent nearly every day together.

I turned and looked at him.

"What's this really about?" I asked, wanting the truth. Did he need something? Was he in trouble? Was this something that Charlie couldn't know about?

A million different things were slamming through my head.

Oh God. What if this has to do with Dex fucking someone Charlie had been with?

I didn't know how that really worked, but I assumed it would still be fucked up in guy code.

I shook my head, not sure what I'd say or do if that was the case. Hell, that's probably why he was acting all interested in me ... he needed my help.

And maybe I'm just reaching here? Maybe this has nothing more to do than him wanting to hang out with me?

I stared at the lake, the silence stretching. However, it wasn't an uncomfortable one.

"This really is about me wanting to talk."

I looked at him after he spoke. He was watching me intently, the shadows playing across his face. He looked dangerous, in a way, but I liked that.

"That's the truth, Eva."

I heard the sincerity in his voice. Everything in me was on high alert, and just being beside Dex, smelling the heady, masculine scent of his cologne filled my head, made me dizzy.

I was also a little ashamed to admit I was aroused. It had always been like this, though. He'd just walk by and I'd smell him, see the muscles rippling under his clothes, and I'd instantly want him.

"Okay, so what should be talk about?" I tried to sound like this was normal, and although we'd had plenty of talks over the years, this felt different.

This felt intimate.

"How have you been?" he asked, his focus still on me.

I shrugged. "Fine, I guess, if working at the bar and having to beat off the drunks is an accomplishment." I was teasing, but I saw the dark look crossing over his face with each passing second.

"You shouldn't work there," he said, his voice hard.

I smiled, hoping to lighten things. "I was just kidding."

He didn't look convinced.

"Besides, I can handle myself; you know that."

He looked at the lake and I saw his clenched jaw. "Yeah, I know that, but if motherfuckers are bothering you—"

I placed my hand on his forearm, his skin warm, his muscles tense. "Hey," I said softly and waited for him to look at me. "I can handle myself. And if they get out of hand, you know Jarren won't stand for that."

He stared into my eyes for long seconds, not speaking, but even just having his gaze on me I felt like he was stroking his fingers along my bare flesh.

"Yeah, I know, but I still don't like it." He looked down at my hand on his arm, and I was embarrassed I was still touching him. But before I could move it away, he placed his much bigger had over mine. "No, keep it there. I like the way it feels."

God, my heart jumped right into my throat.

I probably should have removed my hand anyway, but I liked the feel of his muscles tensing beneath my palm. I'd caused that, and I could see that reality written on his face. I felt it in the way he tightened his hand on mine.

"You know I always noticed you, Eva."

The way he said those words had my heart stopping a little bit. I knew what *I* wanted him to mean, but that didn't mean that's what this was about.

"I noticed you, too," I said, smiling, but knowing it didn't really reach my eyes.

He didn't speak for long seconds, and as the air between us became heated, thick, I had a very real feeling Dex meant something more ... intimate.

He slowly shook his head, and my throat tightened further.

"Do you understand what I mean?" His voice sounded thick, serious.

I didn't answer, because I didn't know if I wanted to admit anything, at least not right now.

"I've *noticed* you ... for years." His voice was low, soft even.

He leaned in just an inch, and I felt the light puffs of his cinnamon breath brush across my lips. A tingling settled over me, and I had this strange feeling Dex might try to kiss me. And when he lowered his gaze to my mouth, something in me shifted.

I wanted his mouth pressed to mine.

I wanted his tongue moving along mine.

I wanted to be in his bed, under him, with that massive cock I knew he had deep inside of me.

God.

But despite wanting this, fear took hold. I didn't know why I was scared as hell, but either way I tensed. Dex must have sensed that from me because he backed off an inch.

"I..."

What in the hell was I supposed to say? Wasn't this what I'd wanted, to have Dex interested in me?

But instead of embracing it, I was afraid of my own feelings.

"I should probably go." I got off the hood of the car, my legs feeling like they were made of pudding, and my mind swirling with this small exchange. Nothing had even happened, yet I was running.

"Eva," Dex called out, his voice deep but firm. I looked at him and watched as he came closer. God, I wanted him to touch me again. I wanted him to look at my mouth as if he was starving to kiss me.

"You're okay?" he asked, genuine worry in his voice.

"I'm fine. It's just late, and I should be getting home."

"I'll follow you, make sure you get home safely."

"You don't have to." I was trying in vain to keep the shakiness from my voice. I was so aroused, so wet, so needy, that it was hard to even think straight right now.

"I know." He took a step closer. "But I'm going to follow you home and make sure you get in okay." There was this hardness in his voice, this "I'm not taking no for an answer" tone.

I nodded, feeling good that he was firm, that he wasn't letting me back down so easy. Call me weak, but I liked that ... loved that.

"Dex—"

"Don't fight me, Eva."

The way he said that had all these thoughts running through my head.

"Don't fight me while I'm deep inside of you and you're begging for more."

"Don't fight me when I have your hands pinned above your head and I'm owning every part of you."

"Don't fight me as I love you, Eva."

"I won't fight you," I whispered, and I watched as his nostrils flared slightly, as if my words had gone deep inside of him ... as if that's just what he wanted to hear.

"Come on. Let's get you home."

I followed him over to my car, where he opened the door for me. When I bent down to climb in, I swear I heard him inhale deeply right by my hair. This shiver worked its way through me. I looked up at him once I was seated in the driver's seat. I saw how tightly he held onto the door, so much that his knuckles were white. I wished I knew what he was thinking.

"I'll be right behind you." He shut the door, and I sat there thinking about what in the hell was going on.

This felt different, and I didn't know if that was a good or a bad thing.

Chapter Four

Dex

I'd wanted to stay at the lake longer, talk more with her, but I could see I was freaking her the fuck out.

Hell, if she knew what I really wanted with her, to do to her, she'd probably run for the fucking hills.

But that wasn't going to stop me from going through with this and telling her exactly how I felt and what I wanted.

I pulled into her driveway, right behind her car, and cut the engine. Maybe I should have just watched her walk in the house and drive off, but I wanted Eva like a fucking fiend needing a fix, and there was no point in waiting to tell her any of this.

I cut the engine and got out at the same time she did. She looked genuinely surprised, but I could also see she was a little happy to see I hadn't just driven off.

"I can get in the house okay." She smiled, and fuck, did it do something nice to my chest.

"I know you can, but just driving off would have been a bastard thing to do, yeah?"

She didn't respond, but started looking nervous. I knew she wanted me, and pretty badly, given the way she'd responded to the little touch I'd given her, the words I'd said, and the fact she'd retreated right before I started to kiss her.

Yeah, this was pretty strange for her, no doubt, but it was right, and I just needed to show her that.

I needed to prove that to her.

She turned and started making her way up to the front door. I knew I should have given her room, but I couldn't fucking help myself. She suddenly stopped, turned, and this hard look crossed her face.

"Dex, I don't know what in the hell is going on, or if you're going through some kind of phase—"

"Phase?" I lifted an eyebrow, knowing my amusement was clear.

She nodded, trying to appear so strong.

It turned me on.

"Yeah, like you've run through all the women in town and I'm the last resort." Her voice was shaky. "Or trying to fuck your friend's sister."

I was getting annoyed, not because she was bringing any of this up, but because she must actually find truth in some of it.

"You think I sleep around?"

She didn't answer, but started biting her lip.

"You think I want to fuck you because it's some kind of notch on my belt? Like it turns me on because you're my fucking best friend's little sister?"

Again, she said nothing. I took a step closer. "I haven't been with a woman in so long it would be embarrassing if I gave a fuck, Eva." I looked down at her mouth again. "I haven't been with a woman because I'm not interested in them. I know what I want, have finally realized what I've been missing out on, and I'm done with that bullshit." I moved a step closer, and I had to give it to her, she didn't back down. "And for the record, I'd never betray Charlie that way. When I'm with you it's for the right reasons, understand?"

She didn't respond.

This low, almost animalistic sound came from the back of my throat, and I didn't even try to mask it. It was a fucking testament to how much I wanted Eva right now.

"I don't want any woman but you." I saw her throat work, and although this was probably coming out of left field for her, I wasn't going to sugarcoat anything. "You want me to leave right now?" I waited a heartbeat for her to respond. Finally, she shook her head slowly.

"Dex." She whispered my name, and it sounded so fucking sweet coming from her lips.

"I want you," I said again.

And not just for right now.

I wanted her for the rest of my life.

I moved closer to her and placed a hand on either side of her head, caging her in, making her lean right up against the side of the house. I inhaled deeply, smelling the sweet yet fresh and crisp scent of her. It made my cock rock had.

I leaned in so our faces were only an inch apart.

"You're kind of moving in fast, aren't you?" she asked, trying to sound strong. I could tell she was, but I also heard the tremble in her voice.

I knew, without even touching her, she wanted me. "No, I don't think I'm moving fast at all." I pressed a little closer to her, crowding her, making her know I was serious as a heart attack.

"I don't know what's going on here," she whispered, her eyes wide, her pupils dilated. Oh, she wanted me all right, if her increased breathing and erect nipples were anything to go by. Hell, I could see the hard little tips pushing against the material of her tight top.

"You want me to tell you what's going on, Eva?" She licked her lips, and I lowered my gaze to watch the act. My cock jerked hard, pressing against my zipper, wanting the fuck out.

"Dex." She breathed out my name again, and fuck, it sounded good.

I stared right in her eyes and moved one of my hands closer to her face so I could run my thumb along the curve of her jaw. I felt her shake slightly, and I leaned loser, my lips nearly brushing her ear. "You've been mine for a long fucking time, Eva." I heard her sharp intake of breath. "But I stayed away because that was the right thing to do." I pulled back so I could look into her eyes again. "It was a stupid move; I can admit that." The moment of silence stretched.

"This is insane."

Yeah, it fucking was, but it was the truth. I wasn't going to hide anything from her.

"You've never shown any interest in me." Her voice was so low, hesitant even.

"We weren't close because you're Charlie's baby sister. That was crossing a fucking line." I heard her swallow.

"I'm still Charlie's little sister." She stated the obvious, and I couldn't help but smirk.

"I realized what I've been missing, Eva. It's the fucking truth. Life bitch slapped me, baby." Her eyebrows pulled down a little. "I'm getting old, and I want to settle down. I want a good woman by my side; I want to have a family I can care and provide for." I continued to stroke my thumb along her jawline. "I won't lie. When I first saw you for the gorgeous woman you are, my first reaction was how badly I wanted to fuck you. I wanted to be inside of you, Eva." I shook my head at my words.

Fuck, I'm a bastard.

She inhaled sharply and parted her lips, as if she couldn't get enough air into her body.

I leaned in another inch until our lips were close enough that when I spoke they'd brush together. "But I haven't been with a woman sexually in years, baby. That's the god's honest truth." I stared into her eyes. "And wanting you, but not having the balls to tell you that has been pretty fucking hard." My heart was beating faster, the adrenaline pumping through my veins. "I've jerked off to you so many times, Eva, just thinking about how fucking gorgeous you are, and how much I want you as mine." She sucked in a breath and I found satisfaction in it. "I can admit to being a motherfucker and being too afraid to make a move on you. I can admit to staying away because I didn't want to rock the boat with you and Charlie." She inhaled slowly, but I could see my words were sinking in. "I can admit that not telling you how I felt was the worst fucking mistake I've ever made."

"Dex," she whispered, her warm, sweet smelling breath moving along my mouth and making my cock jerk even harder. "I stayed away, too. I wasn't honest with myself or you either."

God, I wanted her in my life so damn badly. "There's only one woman I want as mine for the rest of my fucking life, Eva." I moved my thumb so I could now brush it along her bottom lip. "There's only one woman I want as the mother of my children." I continued to brush that digit along the swell of her lip. I was transfixed at what I was doing. And when she slipped just the tip of her tongue out and gently ran it along the pad of my thumb, I thought I'd come right then and there.

Christ.

"This is so crazy," she said, but it held no heat, no emotion.

"But it's also so right, Eva baby."

She didn't say anything, but she didn't have to. This was wild, untamed, and felt so fucking good. Damn, I hadn't even been inside of her yet, and I knew it would be the best I'd ever had.

"What if I don't want this ... whatever *this* is?"

I watched her mouth move as she spoke. "You don't want this? You don't want me?"

She shook her head but didn't say anything.

I grinned, but it wasn't one of amusement. "You can claim you don't want this." I leaned in close. "But you and I both know that'll be a fucking lie." I inhaled deeply, smelling the sweet scent that came from her. "I bet if I placed my hand between your legs you'd be wet for me, Eva." I leaned back an inch so she could get a good look at my face. "Are you wet for me, Eva?" I couldn't stop the low growl that left me at the thought she was primed for me, ready to take me into her body.

"Don't you think this is a little fast?" she asked softly and swallowed, obviously trying to seem reasonable. Hell, I was glad one of us could think straight. As it was, I was hard, possessive of her, and ready to take Eva right up against the fucking building.

"I've known you for years," I murmured and glanced at her mouth again.

Fuck, I want to kiss her.

"It was never like this, Dex."

"It should have been." I closed my eyes and groaned. "Say my name again." She was silent a second, and I looked at her again.

I felt her breath tease my face. "I like hearing it come from your mouth."

She didn't speak for long seconds, but that was okay. For her I'd wait for the rest of my fucking life.

"Dex, we should stop," she said, but there was no heat behind her words. She didn't mean them.

"If you truly want me to stop, then all you have to do is tell the truth, Eva. Don't fucking lie. If you don't want me, don't want this—"

"And what is *this*, Dex?" she said, cutting me off.

I lifted my hand and pushed the long fall of her hair away from her neck. "What I want is you, Eva. I want every part of you as mine. Only mine." I ran my finger along the side of her throat. Her pulse beat wildly beneath her ear, a testament to how worked up she was.

"And you just came to this realization?" she whispered.

I shook my head slowly. I pressed my rock hard cock against her belly. "I just realized I was a fucking fool to try and ignore what I wanted."

"What you wanted…" She didn't phrase it like a question.

"You, Eva." I ground my erection against her. "You feel that?" I asked, but she didn't respond, just licked her lips. I could see the truth in her eyes. "Just tell me you want to be mine."

She parted her lips, but didn't speak. She was nervous, and I couldn't blame her for that. I was coming on pretty fucking strong, but it was like something had snapped in me. I couldn't wait, couldn't try and go slow and easy, even if she deserved that and so much more.

I leaned in close again so my mouth was by her ear now. "I want everyone to know you're mine."

She was breathing harder, faster, and I doubted she'd relax. Her hands were on my biceps, her nails digging into my flesh.

"When I say I want you as mine, I mean that and so much more, Eva." I slipped my hand along her side. Being a bold motherfucker, I placed my palm right between her legs. The skirt she wore gave way, and I growled low at the fact her panties were damp. "I want to own this sweet pussy, Eva."

She made the sweetest little mewling noise.

I nipped at her earlobe, and she dug her nails harder into my flesh. I added just a bit of pressure, but before I snapped at the pleasure I felt and took her right here, I moved my hand back up and placed my open palm right over her belly. My fingers spanned the width, and I leaned back to look in her eyes. "And every single time I take you, claim you as mine, Eva, I'll make sure to fill you up with my cum until you carry my baby."

She gasped.

"I don't want any other woman, don't want any other female to carry my baby." She didn't speak, but she sucked in a breath. "I want to fuck you with nothing between us. I want to be so far in you, so damn deep, that when I fill you up my seed comes out of you days later."

"Oh. God. Dex."

"I want my baby growing right here." I added a little pressure to her belly and watched her chest rise and fall rapidly. "Do you understand exactly what I'm saying?"

She licked her lips and nodded slowly.

"What do you think about that? How does that make you feel?"

She just shook her head, her whole body tight, her pupils still dilated, indicating how aroused she was.

"It scares me."

"But in a good way, doesn't it?"

She closed her eyes and exhaled. "God. Yes."

I grinned even though she couldn't see me.

Yeah, she was right here with me.

Chapter Five

Eva

God, is this really happening?

Dex had his hand on my belly, and I couldn't deny what he said thrilled me, but it also scared the hell out of me.

He wanted me to have his baby.

He wanted me to be his woman.

Yeah, it scared me, and in a good way.

I'd wanted Dex for a long time, but I kept that hidden, moving on with my life. I wasn't going to pine over a man that never saw me as anything more than Charlie's little sister.

I pretended not to pine.

"Tell me you don't want this and I'll leave." His breath brushed along my cheek. He smelled good, clean, manly. "It'll be hard as fuck, Eva, but I'll walk away."

The look in his eyes said he wouldn't give up that easily, and I knew that throughout the years when he'd wanted something he went for it.

Can I do this? Can I really give myself to Dex in all the ways he wants?

It was certainly what I'd wanted ... him, a family, and a life where I could actually be happy. I wasn't thinking about what Charlie might say, or thinking about what was right or wrong.

I was staring into Dex's eyes and seeing the desire, the need he had for me, reflected back, and all common sense and rational thoughts left me.

"I do want you."

He smirked, just a lift at the corner of his mouth. But damn, was it sexy.

He leaned in and claimed my mouth without saying anything in response. The way he stroked his tongue along mine sent this heat wave through my body. When he pulled away, I couldn't breathe. I was ready for him, so ready my panties were wet.

I would have agreed to anything right then and there.

But Dex stepped away when I thought he'd push this more. He smoothed a hand over my cheek, and leaned in once more to kiss me softly on my lips.

"Tomorrow I'm taking you out, Eva," he said quietly, his voice deep. "I'm going to treat you like a real woman, make you know how special you are." He ran the pad of his thumb along my bottom lip, his focus on my mouth still. "As much as I want you, and you better believe I fucking want you—" He reached down and ran a hand over the huge bulge pressing against his jeans. "—We need to start this off right, yeah?"

I nodded, not knowing what else to say.

"God, it's really fucking hard walking away right now, but I don't want to be a bastard. I don't want our first time to be me fucking you up against a wall ... even if that's what I want right now."

I knew he was hard, had felt it pressed against my belly. I wanted to tell him I didn't care as long as he was with me right now. But I bit my lip and stayed still.

"Until tomorrow, baby." He turned and left.

I could only stand there and watch him leave. Right before he got into his vehicle, he turned and looked at me. The way he winked had my pussy clenching painfully.

I wanted him, and I knew when I told him that it sealed my fate.

But was I ready to be the woman Dex wanted? Was I ready to give him what he wanted?

Eva

The following evening

"You're going out with who?" Charlie asked, although he knew damn well.

I looked over at him. I was in the bathroom, getting ready for the dinner Dex had planned for us, and feeling all kinds of nervous.

"Dex," I said again. "I told you that on the phone, you know, right before you came over here."

Charlie had always been protective of me, even when we were younger, and I knew that's what he was doing now. It might be Dex, his best friend, but it was still a guy I was going out with. It being Dex just made it a little more complicated.

"Why?" Charlie asked and leaned against the doorway. He crossed his arms over his chest and just glared at me. I felt like my dad was interrogating me.

"Because he asked." I took a deep breath. "And I like him, Charlie."

My brother didn't say anything, and when I looked at him I saw this intense look on his face. "He's kind of old, yeah?"

I couldn't help it. I started laughing. "He's the same age as you." When Charlie doesn't say anything, I continued. "He's only ten years older than me." Charlie remained silent. I turned and faced my brother. "I mean, are you okay with me having dinner with him?" I wouldn't cancel my plans if Charlie wasn't because I was an adult, but I also didn't want this to be weird.

"Honestly?" he asked, not moving from his position and his focus intense.

"Yeah, of course."

He exhaled softly, his eyes trained on mine. "If there was one guy I'd want you to be with, it would be Dex."

Okay, that threw me for a little bit of a loop. "Really?" My eyebrows knitted, the tightness in my face letting him know my confusion was clear.

"I mean, he's no saint, but there's no one that'll look after you better than he will."

That made me feel all tingly, knowing Charlie approved of Dex and me, and even if he'd said a lot of intense things the other night, I didn't want to let this control me. I had to stay in reality; I knew if I let myself really go off the deep end, the fall would be devastating.

I looked down, my thoughts full of all the things that could go wrong. "I've cared about him for a long time." When I didn't get a response, I looked up at Charlie again.

"I know, Eva," he said softly. "I'm not blind. I've never been blind to the way you look at him ... and the way he's looked at you."

There I was, going through a loop again. "You did? He did?" I thought I'd kept how I felt to myself, but apparently not.

"You and Dex are both transparent as hell."

I felt my cheeks heat at this revelation, but it felt right, good even. "I thought this would bother you, even if it's only dinner."

Charlie shook his head. "It's not just dinner, not to him, Eva. I know Dex, and he doesn't do this kind of shit."

I didn't speak because I didn't know what to say.

"Hell, he hasn't been with a woman in a long damn time, and even before then he didn't sleep around. He always seemed distant in that regard."

Although I didn't want to really hear about Dex and anything he did with other women in the past, hearing that he hadn't been this major manwhore straight from Charlie felt really good.

It's not like I'd been celibate, but knowing Dex hadn't been with woman in a long time made me feel like things were going in the right direction. Maybe that was stupid of me, but if shit hit the fan, I'd deal with it then. Until that time—if that even happened—I was going to just roll with this.

Chapter Six

Dex

We left the bar, but I wasn't damn near done with the night, and I hoped she wasn't either. I held the door open for her, and she stepped out of the restaurant. I wasn't about to deny myself and didn't give a fuck who saw ... I leaned in and inhaled the sweet scent that always clung to her.

I followed her out, and we walked in silence to the car. I was glad she'd let me pick her up. Eva could be headstrong, but if we were doing this, then I wanted to do it right.

"Let me get that," I said and unlocked the passenger side door for her. I held it open, watched her climb in, and saw a blush stealing over her cheeks. Truth was I wanted to be a gentleman with her, but I also wanted her so fucking badly. Doing something like holding the car door open let me watch her long legs fold into the car as she got in. It allowed me to see the slight rise of her skirt as she shifted on the seat.

It allowed me to get my fill of her.

I must have stood there for too long, because she looked up at me. "You got it engrained in your memory?" she said, but I heard the teasing note in her voice.

I cleared my throat. I didn't get embarrassed very often, but having Eva call me out on checking her out had done just that. I closed the door and walked around the car, my cock hard, but there was no way I was hiding the fucker. I didn't want tonight to be about her thinking all I wanted was a fuck.

I wanted her, of course. But this was about us connecting on a deeper level. I hadn't lied or sugarcoated what I wanted with her.

I wanted my baby in her.

I wanted her as my woman.

I wanted her as only mine.

But that didn't mean I wanted her to think all I wanted was between her legs because she could see my fucking hard-on.

I just needed to prove to her that I was right for her.

I needed to prove to Eva that I deserved her.

Eva

I looked over at Dex. He had one hand on the steering wheel, the other on the gearshift, and God, did it look sexy. The short-sleeved shirt he wore showed off his forearms, biceps, and tattoos. I'd always had a thing for muscular arms.

And he has arm porn going on for days.

I shifted slightly as my arousal rose. The entire time at dinner Dex watched me. He'd wanted me to talk about myself, to tell him things he didn't know.

He'd said he wanted to know everything about me.

And he'd been such an intense listener. I knew he heard every word I'd said, and although I'd never had anyone that interested in what I had to say, it felt good.

He was heading back to my house, and although he'd told me during dinner he was having a good time, he'd never pushed keeping the night going on longer.

But I wanted it to. God, I really wanted it to.

I didn't need to know every little detail about Dex to know what I wanted, and that was him, in every raw, hardened form he presented.

But even if we'd known each other for years, could I really be bold and tell him what I wanted, or how I really wanted this night to end?

I faced forward and swallowed.

"You know, even if you had told me to fuck off, I would have still tried, Eva."

I looked over at him, not really surprised. I knew Dex well enough that if he wanted something he went after it.

He didn't look at me, but I saw him smirk, and God, did it turn me on.

"Yeah, I know you well enough." I couldn't help but smile, too. We rode for another ten minutes before he pulled up in front of my house. I wasn't sure exactly what to say, but when I turned to face him, maybe to say good night, or hell, maybe to invite him in, Dex had his hand on the back of my neck and pulled me forward.

He kissed me hard, possessive, and as I rested one of my hands on his thighs, and the other on his shoulder to balance myself, all I felt was this intense need to be with him.

The feeling of his tongue moving in and out of my mouth, pressing against my tongue, had my pussy so wet I couldn't even breathe. But when he pulled me on top of him, I could feel the huge hardness of what was between his thighs. He wanted me; that was clear.

He pulled away just enough that we weren't kissing anymore, but our lips were still touching. "If I put my hand between your legs and touched your pussy, would you be wet for me, Eva?" he whispered against my mouth, and I breathed harder.

"I don't know, maybe you should find out." I was feeling pretty damn bold right now. I felt him smile against my mouth, but he didn't make a move to touch me. Instead, he took hold of my wrist in his hand and placed my palm flat on my chest.

"Show me, Eva."

I sucked in a lungful of air and slowly moved my hand down my body. He still had a hold on my wrist as I descended. Lower I went, our focus on each other. I stopped at my lower belly.

"Keep going, Eva." There was this fire behind his eyes, something that had me burning brighter, and I was about to get singed. But I didn't care.

I pushed my hand underneath my skirt, and as soon as I was under the material, he let go of my wrist and placed his fingers on my panties. I groaned, he closed his eyes, and together we blew out ragged breaths.

He rubbed me gently over my panties at first, but the longer he did that, and the more the seconds moved by, the faster he went. He was right over my clit, moving his finger back and forth over the swollen bud, and I knew I could come right then and there.

"Tell me what you want, Eva. Tell me and it's yours." His voice was so damn gruff. "Even if it's goodnight, I'll fucking take my hand away and kiss you goodnight."

"Is that what you want?" I pressed my lower body an inch down and rubbed my pussy back and forth over his hand, wanting to come desperately.

Dex didn't answer verbally. He just shook his head slowly.

"Tell me what *you* want," I whispered.

He didn't answer for long seconds, but he did keep rubbing me, making me suffer in the most incredible way.

"Dex—"

"The things I want to do to you are pretty fucking filthy, baby." He leaned in an inch and pressed his mouth firmly against mine again. He ran his tongue over my bottom lip and I shivered, feeling that pleasure build inside of me. "Do you want to come on top of me while we're parked in front of your house and I have my hand up your skirt?"

I wanted to say yes, that it really didn't matter where I was as long as he kept doing what he was doing. But, before I could say anything, he was speaking again.

"Or do you want to get off with my big dick shoved up your tight little pussy?"

Oh. God.

"You want to feel me filling you up with my cum, making you slick and hot from it?"

I moaned.

"You want me to make you feel so good you won't want anyone else but me?"

He stopped rubbing and pulled back. I forced my eyes open, looked at him, and tried to form a coherent thought.

We stared at each other for several seconds, both of our breathing jagged, the windows becoming steamy.

"You want my cock in you, don't you, baby?"

I nodded.

I wasn't even about to lie.

Chapter Seven

Eva

After I'd nodded, Dex hadn't wasted any time getting us into the house.

I kicked the front door shut with my foot, and Dex had me pressed up against the wall a second later.

"I want to be so deep in you, Eva," he groaned against my neck, and I turned my head and gave him better access.

He had his hands on either side of my head, caging me in, making me feel trapped, but in a good way.

"I want to pump you so full of my cum it comes out of you and makes your panties wet the next day."

"Dex. God," I breathed out.

"I want you so sore that when you sit down tomorrow all you can feel is me still inside you, Eva."

I didn't know if an orgasm could actually happen just from hearing someone talk dirty, but I'd find out soon enough.

He lowered his gaze to my mouth, his chest brushing along mine. "Being mine means you're my everything."

God, for such a strong, hardened man, Dex knew how exactly what to say to make me fall even harder.

I lowered my gaze to his mouth, my lips still tingling. "You sure you want to go there with me?" I whispered.

He lowered his head an inch closer to me. "Oh, yeah." He kissed me then, hard, possessively, demanding more. He started pressing his erection against my belly. He was huge, long, and so hard it was like he was sporting a steel pipe between his legs. "I want all of you, Eva," he murmured against my mouth.

I was more than willing to give all of myself to him.

He moved his hands down my face, stroked his fingers along the sides of my neck, and stopped right below my ears. Dex placed his thumbs at my pulse points, adding just the slightest pressure. It was so strange, but that small touch made everything in me come alive even more.

After a few seconds, he continued to descend my body. He stroked his tongue over my lips for only a second before delving into my mouth. When he was at my hips, he curled his fingers into my flesh and pulled me hard against him. I gasped, and his cock dug into my belly even harder.

He broke the kiss and started moving his mouth down my neck, stopping at my collarbone. When he ran his tongue over the bone, I shivered and dug my nails into his shoulders He hissed, but then groaned.

"That's it, baby. Give me more."

I breathed out heavily. I was so damn wet my panties were soaked clear through. A shiver worked its way through me when he went back to licking at my skin. It was like he was this wild animal.

My wild animal, and all this feral attention is for me.

"Touch me more, Eva."

I grabbed his head, tangled my fingers in his long hair, and pulled at the strands. He hissed out and lifted his head so we were eye level. A second passed with silence between us.

"Do it again," he gritted out.

I tugged at the strands hard enough his head went back and the tendons in his throat stood out in stark relief. But his eyes were locked on mine.

"You're so fucking hot," he said right before he slammed his mouth on mine. Our teeth clashed, our tongues fucked, and I was more than ready for whatever Dex wanted.

When he broke away this time, he flared his nostrils for a second. I could see his mouth parted, his pupils dilated.

He's going to lose it, and it's all because of me.

I started breathing harder at that thought. It was like I was looking into the face of a feral animal that was about to snap.

I was the one to lean in and kiss him this time, and he groaned into my mouth. Dex grabbed my hair, and the force with which he pulled my hair had the pain mixing with pleasure.

After long seconds, he finally broke the kiss, and I wanted to beg him to fuck me already.

He rested his forehead against mine, our breath mingling. "I'm going to fuck you so hard, Eva."

He was rock hard, so big and thick. I was so aroused that wetness coated my inner thighs. Dex smoothed his hands over my ass, ran the pads of his index fingers along the crease where my butt and legs met, and then moved lower down the back of my thighs. He moved back up, and in the next second, he had my skirt and panties clean off of me.

I stood there, not sure what to do now, but Dex had plans, because he had my shirt pulled up and over my head. He tossed it to the ground and, in a matter of seconds, had my bra off, too.

Here I was, naked, aching, so damn wet, and ready for Dex to have his way with me.

My throat was so dry, but I managed to say, "Touch me."

He didn't make me wait. Dex placed his hand right between my thighs. His fingers were so big, slightly calloused, and I closed my eyes and exhaled roughly. He dipped his head and ran his tongue along my nipple, making the tip harder, more sensitive.

He alternated between breasts for long minutes, all the while touching my pussy.

"Dex," I whispered and closed my eyes as his fingers found my swollen clit. He ran small circles around the bud then went back to rubbing his finger through my cleft.

He touched me for a few seconds, sucked and kissed at my skin until I was trembling, but before I could come, he stopped and stepped several feet back. I watched in rapt attention as he licked his fingers, sucking off my wetness.

"So fucking sweet," he growled. "You've always been mine, Eva." His head was downcast, but his eyes were locked on me. "I was just too much of a fucking idiot to accept it."

Power and strength radiated from him. I took in the wide expanse of his broad shoulders, followed the lines of his tattoos that wrapped around his arms and chest, and felt my heart jerk in my chest.

"You ready for me?"

I lowered my gaze, taking in that V of muscle that was starkly defined. He might have his pants on, but his erection pushed at the fabric. It was huge, and I could only imagine what it would look like once it was freed.

I nodded.

I was more than ready.

Chapter Eight

Dex

There was nothing more I wanted in this world than the woman in front of me.

She's mine.

I felt like a fucking animal with her right now. Looking my fill of her naked body, my cock jerked at the sight. I wanted to fucking jerk off and just watch her, just see her smooth her hands over her body, those long fingers moving over the intimate parts of her. But I'd have plenty of time to take in every part of her ... memorize every single inch.

I saw her throat work as she swallowed. She was worked up, so fucking primed for me I knew if I touched her in just the right way she'd come for me.

I wanted her unhinged, but I also wanted to take my time, to make this last.

Yeah. Fuck. Right.

There was no way I was going to last tonight, not once I was deep in her pretty cunt.

"You're looking at me like you're starving," she whispered, her chest rising and falling as she breathed harder.

I growled low. Yeah, when it came to Eva, I was a fucking animal.

"I am, Eva." I moved an inch closer. "I'm so fucking hungry for you." I put my hand on her belly; her body trembled for me. "I want to put my baby in here. Right. Fucking. Here." She swallowed again, and I watched the line of her throat work through the act. "You want that, don't you?" I wanted to hear her say she wanted me to put my baby inside her. "Tell me how much you want to be mine. Tell me how much you want to be pregnant with my baby."

She closed her eyes and moaned.

"Look at me," I demanded and gripped her chin in my fingers.

She opened her eyes, her pupils fully dilated. "I want your baby in me. I want to be yours in every way."

Jesus.

It took all of my control not to fucking come right in my jeans.

Eva licked her lips, and I was riveted to the sight. The dirty images of her on her knees, with her mouth wrapped around my dick, slammed into my head. I was big, my cock thick and long, and she'd have a hard time working her mouth down all of it. But fuck, yeah, that would be hot.

I leaned forward and ran my tongue along the seam of her lips. I could easily become addicted to her.

I'm already fucking addicted to Eva.

"I am so damn hard for you."

She made this soft noise, one that sounded like need and desperation and everything that turned me on. I slipped my hand behind her nape, curled my finger into her soft flesh, and tilted her head to the side. I leaned down and ran my tongue along the side of her throat, feeling her pulse jack up higher.

"I'll make you feel so fucking good."

"You already are, Dex." She made another small noise and dug her nails into my skin. My cock jerked at the pleasure and pain.

I wanted this first time to be romantic, but I knew I couldn't go slowly with her. Hell, having her pressed up against the wall and dry humping the fuck out of her was hard as hell.

I dragged my hand up her belly and over her ribcage to cup one of her big breasts. I pushed my pelvis forward, grinding my jean-clad cock into her softness. I didn't move for long seconds, my thoughts becoming pretty damn real.

"I wish we'd gotten together years ago," I said softly, meaning it down to my fucking marrow. I looked into her eyes, hoping she wasn't getting freaked the fuck out by what I said.

"Me too, Dex."

I closed my eyes; that thrill of pleasure had nothing to do with sexual gratification moving through me.

"We have now, though," she said.

"We have forever." I went back to sucking on her neck, dragging my tongue up the slender column of her throat, and I thrust my cock against her belly, back and forth, needing that friction, that closeness. Pulling back was hard as hell, but I managed to do it, because I needed to be inside her.

"As much as foreplay sounds pretty fucking incredible, I need to shove my nine inches into you, Eva."

I should have some kind of fucking control, or at least try and have it.

Here she was for me, naked, ready...

I had her in my arms a second later, strode to the bedroom, and kicked the door shut with my foot. When she was on the center of the bed, her legs slightly parted, her pussy a little hidden from me because it was dark in the room, I took a deep, steadying breath.

Control. I need to keep my fucking control.

"Take off your clothes," Eva whispered in this sultry voice.

I got the fuck out of my clothes, needing to be just as bare as she was. While looking at her body, taking in the long lines with shadows covering them, the rise of her large breasts, the dip and arch of her hips, I reached down and grabbed my cock. Her legs were long, smooth. Even her fucking feet were hot as shit.

I started stroking myself from root to tip, unable to control myself like some kind of teenager. But when I was around Eva, and especially now that she was giving herself to me, I didn't want to keep my control.

The tip of my dick was wet with pre-cum, and I ran my palm over the crest, my whole body tight.

"Show yourself to me, Eva." I didn't even try to mask the urgency or intensity in my voice. "I want to see what I'll be fucking owning tonight." And as she obeyed me instantly, all I could do was watch in rapt awe. "I meant what I said. Every. Fucking. Word."

I knew she was well aware of what I wanted with her. I'd made no secret of it. And if she had told me to stop, or she didn't want this, I would have backed the fuck off.

But instead of telling me that this was all too unreal, and that I'd lost my fucking mind, she breathed in and out slowly and said, "I know. It's what I want, too, Dex." She reached down, spread her pussy lips wide, and showed me exactly what was mine.

This was my woman, and together we'd make a baby, no matter how many times it took.

Hell, I was looking forward to it.

Chapter Nine

Eva

"Touch yourself for me," Dex said in this low, husky voice.

I parted my legs even wider, if that was possible, and touched myself, showed him the most intimate part of me. I wanted to make him feel good, wanted to please him. It wasn't a weakness, but a power.

I looked down at the long, thick length of his cock, and he was rock hard for me.

He was huge.

He stroked himself in slow motion. It was like he was always watching me, always keeping his attention laser-focused on me.

"You like watching me fucking jerk off? You like knowing what you do to me?"

I nodded, not finding my voice.

It was dark in the room, but I could clearly see the pre-cum coming out of the tip of his cock.

"This," he said and ran the tip of his finger over the crown of his cock, gathering that clear fluid, "will soon be in you."

My heart jumped into my throat. *I want that.*

"I'm going to pump so much cum into you the sheets will be wet because of it." He took a step closer. "But you want that, don't you?"

I nodded again and continued to run my finger up and down my slit, my body ready to take him.

He took a step closer until he was at the edge of the bed, his focus on my splayed thighs, watching me touch myself. I moved my finger to my clit and started rubbing the bud. A gasp left me as the pleasure slammed into me. Here we were, watching each other pleasure ourselves, and it was so damn erotic.

Dex stroked himself a little faster, the sound of his hand moving over his length, of flesh slapping against flesh, filling my head. His bicep contracted and relaxed from the rapid motion of jerking off.

"I could get off just watching you touch yourself, Eva." He groaned, took his hand off his dick, and finally moved onto the bed with me. He placed his hands beside my head and looked down the length of my body.

"I want this so badly," I said before I could stop myself.

"*I* want you so fucking badly," he said and looked at my face. He hovered above me, his huge body looming over me, making me feel so very feminine.

"After tonight, there's no going back."

I didn't want to.

"After tonight, you're finally mine." He leaned in close, but didn't kiss me. "Tonight, I finally claim you, Eva."

"I've always been yours," I said without realizing it, even if we'd gone our separate ways over the years. That didn't matter because we were here now, together. But the words were already out, and I could see they made Dex happy.

Kiss me.

Maybe he needed it as much as I did, or that I'd said it out loud, but Dex had his mouth on mine seconds later. I couldn't stop the small noise that left the back of my throat. And it was as if that sound made something in Dex snap, because he made this distorted sound, grabbed a chunk of my hair behind my head, and jerked my head back.

With my head back, my throat arched, bared, he started to kiss and suck the side of my neck again. He was thorough with his tongue and lips, making me squirm beneath him, ready to beg for his cock in me.

I felt the hot, hard length of him press between my thighs, right through my slit. He started moving his hips back and forth, rubbing himself through my clit.

I looked down as much as I could, and with the way Dex hovered over me, I could see his cock sliding through my cleft. It was so arousing, and I knew I could get off from this alone.

His cockhead moved against my clit every time he pressed his dick upward. I groaned at how good it felt.

"How much do you want me in you?" he whispered by my ear.

I wanted to feel him stretching me, pushing into me hard, demandingly. I wanted to feel like I'd split in two.

"You know how much I want it."

Dex didn't say anything else; he just started to swirl his tongue around the shell of my ear, causing my lips to part and my eyes to close.

Without breaking away, he reached between our bodies, grabbed his cock, and placed the tip at the entrance of my pussy. Everything inside of me stilled, tensed. He pulled back so our faces were an inch apart. For long seconds, he did nothing but stare into my eyes, his cock poised right there. If I just shifted, I could impale myself on him.

"I can't go slow, and there is no going back, Eva."

All I could do was nod. I didn't want slow, and I didn't want to go back. I just wanted us to move forward.

In one, deep, hard thrust, he shoved all those huge inches into me. My back arched, and my breasts were thrust out. He groaned above me, closed his eyes, and I saw, felt, how taut his body became. His balls were pressed right up against my body as he buried himself all the way in me. I was stretched to the max, the pain mixing with the pleasure, making me hungry for more.

When he started moving in and out, faster and harder with each passing second, I didn't stop myself from grabbing onto his biceps. Perspiration covered both of us in thick droplets. His massive chest rose and fell as he breathed, pumping in and out of me.

"Fuck," he said harshly. He pushed in and pulled out, over and over, groaning with every thrust and retreat.

I wanted to see what he was doing, so I lifted up on my elbows and looked down the length of my body. I saw his cock moving in and out of me, glossy from my juices.

I lifted my gaze to his abdomen, seeing his six-pack clench and relax with every thrust he made into me. "You like watching me fuck you?" he asked, sounding out of breath.

When I couldn't hold myself up anymore because he was making me feel so good, I fell backward. Once I hit the mattress, it was as if something shifted in Dex. He went primal on me then. His pelvis slapped against mine, the sound of sloppy sex so fucking arousing.

He pulled out, and I gasped in surprise and disappointment, but Dex flipped me over onto my belly, smoothed his hand along the side of my body, and made this low sound of need.

He didn't make me wait long to shove those nine inches into me again. Dex palmed my ass with his big hands and gripped the mounds almost painfully.

God, that feels good.

"So fucking perfect." He grabbed my waist in a firm hold and hauled me up so I was now on my hands and knees. I felt so bare in this position, but it was the best kind of vulnerability. Dex pushed my legs wider apart with his knee; now my pussy was on full display, my lips parted for him.

He smoothed his hand over my left ass cheek, gently at first, but I wasn't fooled. Dex was raw in every way. He gave my ass a hard spank, and I jerked and gasped in pleasure.

"I'm not going to stop until you're pregnant with my baby, Eva." He ran his hand up my back, right over my spine. "And when my seed takes inside of you, you'll know what it means to be mine."

I'd never get sick of hearing him say how he wanted to get me full with his baby.

Never.

He speared his hand in my hair, yanked my head back, and growled. With his hand in my hair, he used his other one to reach between us and place himself back at my pussy hole. In a fluid motion, he shoved back into my pussy.

"*Jesus,* Eva."

"Oh. God. *Dex.*"

He moved in and out of me slowly, but after a few seconds, he started picking up speed. Soon, his flesh was slapping against mine. He let go of my hair and gripped my hips with both hands, pulling me back on his cock as he surged forward.

He grunted, and my pleasure increased. Dex held my hips so tightly the pain had me gasping out. But it was the pleasure that overrode everything else.

"Fuck. Yeah." He thrust into me once, twice, and on the third stroke, he shoved deep and hard into me before stilling. "God, I'm going to come, baby." His nails dug into my skin, and I came, my pussy clamping down hard on his dick. He filled me up with so much of his seed, I swore I felt it as he came.

"Mine. You're mine forever, Eva." He jerked above me, still coming.

Then, after a few seconds, he covered my back with his chest, and his breath, coming out in hard pants, bathed my flesh in this humid, arousing sensation. Dex pulled out of me, and I couldn't stop myself from collapsing onto the mattress. I breathed hard against the sheets, trying to get my heart to still its rapid rhythm. Dex lay beside me, pulled me close, and placed his hand right between my thighs.

"I want my cum to stay in you, Eva. It belongs inside of you." He kissed the curve of my shoulder.

My skin was damp with perspiration, but it was nice because I knew exactly why I was sweaty. Dex pushed his finger into my pussy, and I shook and moaned.

"I want it inside of you," he murmured as he pushed his seed back into my body when it started slipping out of me.

"God, Eva," he said huskily.

This warm feeling filled me when he leaned down and kissed the top of my head.

I didn't know what the future held, no matter what either of us said, but I knew one thing… this felt pretty damn good.

Maybe this all should have felt more confusing, more insane. But to be honest, it felt like the most perfect thing in the world.

And I didn't want to let that go.

Eva

I lay beside Dex, listening to his deep, even breathing. It could have lulled me to sleep, but I was too deep in thought to get some rest.

I shifted, but he made this deep grunt, rolled over toward me, and wrapped his arm around my waist. He pulled me in close to his hard body, and I melted against him, loving that even in sleep, he wanted me close.

All of this felt so foreign in a sense, but it also felt right, like this was right where I was supposed to be. I lifted my hand and smoothed my fingers over the definition of his biceps. His muscles flexed beneath my touch, and he made this deep sound in his throat, one that sounded like he was thoroughly content and happy.

It's exactly how I feel right now.

I shifted once again so that my chest was pressed to his. He slowly opened his eyes, and if possible, he looked even sexier with that post-sex, hazy look of relaxation covering his face.

"Hey, you," he whispered, his voice so deep, so husky it speared right into me.

"Hey right back." I lifted my hand and cupped his scruff-covered cheek, smoothing my fingers along his face.

"This is real," he said without making it a question.

I stared right into his eyes.

"This is real," he said again and placed his hand on my belly. "Everything I said was the truth, Eva." He leaned in and kissed me, and I felt my heart flutter a bit. "I won't let you go. You're mine."

I'd jumped head first off a cliff, and although I didn't know what the future held, I was looking forward to reaching the bottom ... because I knew Dex would be there.

Chapter Ten

Eva

Five weeks later

I held the plastic bag in my hand, my fingers wrapped tightly around it, and my heart thundering.

Over the last month or so, Dex and I had been inseparable, or rather, Dex hadn't wanted me out of his sight. We spent our free time together, but it wasn't just having incredible sex—even though he was insatiable, and I was more than okay with that. He lavished attention on me, showed me a bad boy could have a softer, gentler side, too.

His protectiveness might not fly with some women, but for me, I was all about it. Heck, his jealousy over a guy even looking at me, the fact he wanted to stake a claim, even if that was glaring at said guy and wrapping his arm around me in ownership made me feel pretty damn wonderful.

"That you, baby?" Dex called out from somewhere in the house, and I took a deep breath. We weren't living together, but I spent a lot of time at his place, and when I wasn't here, he was at my house.

"Yeah," I called out. I didn't want to tell him what I was doing, especially if it came back negative. I don't know why I didn't just come out and tell Dex I was taking a pregnancy test. We never used protection, and we both knew what the result could be because of that.

He was hoping for a baby, and he made no secret of that.

And even though I'd never actually told him I wanted that too ... I did.

I went into the bathroom, shut and locked the door, and pulled out the pregnancy test. Maybe I should have gotten more than one, but I didn't want to be a freak about this. I also didn't want to get his hopes up, or mine for that matter, by saying anything. I'd been late plenty of times in my life, and it had never been because I might have been pregnant.

I read the directions three times, although I was pretty sure this was all self-explanatory. I'd also seen enough movies with chicks peeing on the stick and waiting for the results that I knew the drill. But still, I read the damn pamphlet again and again.

When I pulled out the stick and eyed it, my heart started beating double time.

I did the whole unwrapping, taking the cap off, and before I did the whole peeing on it thing, I stared down at this little white and purple test.

After getting my thoughts as clear as I could, I finished it off, put the cap on, and set it on the counter. While I waited for it to do its thing, I washed and dried my hands and then stared at my reflection. My hair was piled up on my head, the heat making things unbearable. I lowered my gaze to my breasts. They were fuller, so sensitive even wearing a bra was a little uncomfortable.

After I figured enough time had passed, I reached out to take the stick off the counter. My hands shook, and my heart momentarily stopped. I looked down at the little clear window, my throat tightening even further at the results.

Pregnant.

I stared down at it for long seconds, making sure I was reading it correctly. On instinct, I placed a hand on my belly and looked at my reflection again. The woman who stared back at me had wide eyes and a look of shock on her face. It was after the initial surprise left me that I felt excitement.

I was pregnant.

I'm pregnant.

I turned around, unlocked the door, and pulled it open, and standing on the other side was Dex. He looked a little worried, maybe thinking something was wrong since I had hauled ass to the bathroom. But then he looked down at the test I held. A moment of silence passed, almost like time stood still, like this moment was frozen.

I lifted the test up so he could see the window, and although he could read it fine, I was sure, I still said, "I'm pregnant." Those words hung between us, and slowly he looked up from the stick to my face. "I'm pregnant, Dex." My voice was nothing but a whisper, and before I knew what was happening, he had me in his arms.

He had a hand on the back of my head, holding me to his chest. The warmth of his breath moved the hairs on the side of my face. He was tense, and now I was worried maybe something was wrong. Maybe he was having doubts? But before I could move or say anything, he pulled back an inch and looked down at me.

"You're pregnant," he said with a smile on his face, and I felt all the tension leave me.

"Is this crazy?" I asked, but I was smiling, feeling elation finally rise up, when just moment ago, it had been masked by my nervousness.

He cupped my face, stroked his thumbs along my cheeks, and the happiness I saw on his face made me love this man even more.

"You know how much I love you, Eva?" He kept stoking my cheeks, and I knew he wanted me close. I could feel it in his touch. "I love you so fucking much." And surprising the hell out of me once again, Dex dropped to his knees in front of me and rested his forehead on my belly. "My woman. My baby." He pushed my shirt up and kissed the skin below my belly button. He looked up at me, the seriousness on his face evident. "Marry me," he said, and I was speechless.

"We don't have to get married just because I'm pregnant—"

He stood up, interrupting what I was saying. Taking my hand in his, Dex pulled me down the hall to his bedroom. He let go of me, walked over to the dresser, and when he opened it and pulled out a small black ring box, my heart jumped in my throat.

"I don't know when I planned on asking, Eva, but it's not because I wasn't sure." He turned around and showed me the ring. "I've had this for a couple of weeks, but was going to wait longer so it didn't look like I was crowding you." He moved closer to me, and I knew my body was shaking. "I also wanted to make this special, and for you to be sure what you wanted when I asked."

I breathed in sharply.

"I want you, not just as the mother of my baby, but as my wife." He pulled the ring out of the box and slipped it on my finger. "Marry me, Eva. You've already made me the happiest man in the fucking world, but I want *this* so damn badly, too."

I didn't want to cry, but God, I could feel it coming on. He placed his hand on my belly, smiling. "Yes," I whispered. He leaned in and kissed me.

"I think we'll be pretty kickass parents."

"Yeah, I think so, too."

Dex

Four months later

There it was … *my* baby. I squeezed Eva's hand and looked at her. She was staring at the ultrasound monitor. She had this rounded belly, and I wanted to cover her skin, run my hand over the swell. My baby grew in there.

God, I love this woman so much.

"Do you want to know the sex?" the tech asked.

Eva looked at me then. "Do you?" I could hear the excitement in her voice.

I reached out and took her hand, giving it a squeeze, and nodded.

It took a few seconds while the tech was doing more measurements, more typing, but then she pointed to the screen. "Right there," she said and looked at us. "It looks like it's a boy."

My heart jackknifed in my chest, and I looked at Eva. She was smiling from ear to ear.

"We're having a boy," she whispered, and I couldn't stop myself from cupping her face and kissing her. I didn't give a shit if the tech was seeing this PDA. I'd always show my affection when it came to Eva.

The tech started cleaning off the gel from Eva's belly, and when that was done, I placed both hands on either side of her swelled stomach and leaned down to kiss her skin softly. Eva placed her hands in my hair, smoothing her fingers over my scalp.

I turned my face so I could see Eva. "I love you, baby."
She smiled in return. "I love you, too."
God, what I felt for Eva grew every single day.
It was the best fucking feeling in the world.

Epilogue

Dex

Five years later

Life really had no meaning for me without the love of a woman and the laughter of my children filling my head.

And that's what I had.

I was the luckiest fucking man in the world.

I pulled Eva in closer to me, buried my face in her hair, and closed my eyes as I inhaled. She smelled incredible and felt so damn good in my arms. I slipped my arm around her and spanned my open palm on her belly. She was big and round with our fourth child. I was insatiable when it came to her and filling her with my cum; putting my babies inside of her only made me want her more.

I wanted her constantly, and seeing her healthy, glowing, and pregnant with what was mine, had proprietary need and possession claiming me.

She'd always be mine, no matter what.

Eva was due in about a month, and although she was probably sick of me wanting her like a fiend, she always let me have her. But then I made sure I had her coming twice before I got off.

I started rubbing her belly and felt my baby kick. I smiled. God, I loved this. She placed her hand on mine.

"I didn't wake you, did I, baby?"

She hummed softly and turned around to face me, although she made a little grunting noise in the process. "No."

Her sleepy smile had my cock getting hard once more. I knew she could feel it prodding her thigh, but she didn't give me a hard time about my voracious appetite when it came to her.

The years had gone by in a happy blur for me, and I did my best to make sure Eva and my kids were happy, safe, and cared for. I was the provider, and although Eva was more than welcome to work, she preferred staying home with the babies.

I rubbed her belly again, and my little girl kicked again.

"You think you can handle this baby girl, Dex?" She had her eyes closed, but a little smile covered her face.

With Jackson, our five-year-old, and Harlow and Mav, our twin three-year-old boys, this baby girl coming into our lives was another blessing. But it also had every protective instinct coming out full force in me.

"If I can handle you, I can handle anything."

She opened her eyes and chuckled.

"But I do have some ground rules."

She lifted an eyebrow. "Oh yeah?"

"No dating for her until I'm dead." Eva chuckled a little harder. "And if a guy comes to the house asking her out, I'll show him my gun collection right before I break all of his bones."

She started laughing, the sound hitting me right in the chest. Seeing her carefree, even if she thought I was joking, had me feeling so fucking good.

"You don't even own any guns," she finally said, and wiped a tear from the corner of her eye.

"I'm buying stock in an arsenal as soon as she's born." I leaned in for a kiss. I slid my hand along her neck, cupped the side of it, and tilted her head back to really delve inside. She tasted sweet and fruity, and my cock jerked in response. We were both naked, and her big tits pressed against my chest.

"I'm sure the boys will be pretty protective of their baby sister, as well."

I grunted. "They better be."

I started kissing her again, and as the seconds passed, all I thought about was this moment.

"God, I could take you again right here, baby." But I wouldn't because she had to be sore from the loving I'd given her just half an hour ago. I picked up her hand and kissed her ring finger. Her wedding ring scraped against my lips, and I kissed the rock again.

"If I could marry you all over again, I would, baby."

She smiled, her sleepy expression taking on a heated, more aroused look.

"Want to pretend it's our honeymoon again?"

I chuckled, and I was more than willing to give that a go. It might have been years since we'd gotten married, but for me, it felt like the first time every time with her.

This woman and my children were the reason I lived.

I looked down at Eva, seeing the love reflected back at me.

"What?" she whispered after I'd been staring at her for long moments.

"I love you so fucking much." I smoothed my fingers over her cheeks. "I'd die for you. Do you know that?"

She leaned forward an inch and kissed me softly. "I know."

Pushing down the blanket, I exposed her bared, rounded belly. I leaned down, ran my lips along her flesh, and framed her roundness. She ran her fingers over my hair, and I shivered at her touch.

My wife.

My life.

"Are you still happy?" I asked. I asked her this same question often, not because I didn't think she was, but because I loved hearing her response.

"More than I could describe in words."

"You're mine," I said and looked up at her. I pulled her closer and just held her.

There was nothing more important than the woman in my arms, my baby in her belly, or the sons she'd given me.

"It's you." I stroked my fingers along her arm. "It's always been you." I leaned down to kiss the soft skin on her shoulder. "And it'll always be you."

The End

Coming Soon: Experienced

He'll show her how a real man treats a woman...

SABINE

I've never known how good it could feel to be taken care of by a man who knew what he was doing.

Until I was with Hugo...

HUGO

I was older than her.

She was innocent, hadn't experienced all that life had to offer.

I could give her that experience.

Sabine consumed my thoughts, made me desire nothing else but her. No other woman compared to her, and because of that, I haven't been with a woman for four years, which was also the last time I saw Sabine.

But I was done feeling guilty for what I desired. I wanted Sabine in my life, by my side, and I was about to make that a reality.

I didn't know if she'd ever been treated the way a female should ... but I was going to show her how a real man takes care of a woman.

Coming September 2016

Goodreads: http://bit.ly/2aeciBA

About the Author

Want to learn more about Jenika Snow?
Check her out below...

Web: http://www.jenikasnow.com/
Email: Jenika_Snow@yahoo.com
FB: http://www.facebook.com/jenikasnow
Twitter: http://www.twitter.com/jenikasnow
Crescent Snow Publishing:
http://www.crescentsnowpublishing.com

60361091R00111

Made in the USA
Charleston, SC
30 August 2016